R_x

Also by the author

Snow

The Nine Lives of Chloe King series

The Fallen

The Stolen

The Chosen

Tracy Lynn

Simon Pulse

New York   London   Toronto   Sydney   New Delhi

SIMON PULSE

An imprint of Simon & Schuster Children's Publishing Division

1230 Avenue of the Americas, New York, New York 10020

This Simon Pulse edition February 2015

Text copyright © 2006 by Elizabeth J. Braswell

Cover photograph copyright © 2015 by Alamy

All rights reserved, including the right of reproduction in whole or in part in any form.

SIMON PULSE and colophon are registered trademarks of Simon & Schuster, Inc.

For information about special discounts for bulk purchases, please contact Simon & Schuster Special Sales at 1-866-506-1949 or business@simonandschuster.com.

The Simon & Schuster Speakers Bureau can bring authors to your live event. For more information or to book an event contact the Simon & Schuster Speakers Bureau at 1-866-248-3049 or visit our website at www.simonspeakers.com.

Cover design by Russell Gordon

Interior design by Mike Rosamilia

The text of this book was set in Memphis LT Std.

Manufactured in the United States of America

2 4 6 8 10 9 7 5 3 1

Library of Congress Control Number 2005932237

ISBN 978-1-4814-2951-1 (hc)

ISBN 978-1-4814-2950-4 (pbk)

ISBN 978-1-4391-2040-8 (eBook)

This book is for
Maya Rachel Kraske Scotkin.
Your daddy helped me out on this book
in more ways than I can count.

Junior year

1

Vitamin R

Well if they're making it (making it)
Then they're pushing it (pushing it)
—Chevelle

"Cheese!"

A strobe of red followed by a flash of bright white, hopefully bouncing off my teeth and sparkling in my eyes. I tried not to giggle.

"That's it, everyone," the school photographer announced with a smile.

Everyone on the school literary magazine fell forward, now released from our pose. We were all giddy from just having put the spring issue of *Veritas* to rest. Even Will, who just designed the cover, had smiled unexpectedly for the camera. And Meera had actually dressed up. Sort of.

"Congratulations, everyone," Mrs. Tildenhurst said. She put her arm around me and gave me a special squeeze. "I am so sorry you're not going to be with us next year, Thyme. You did such wonderful work."

I blushed a little and felt genuinely bad. "Sorry, I just don't have the time. I think I should concentrate on my strengths my senior year—and unfortunately, they just don't include anything of literary merit." Besides, I had been on the magazine for three years now, and junior year extra-currics counted more than senior for college applications. Or so the legend went.

Tildenhurst gave me an odd look. "That's a funny thing for someone so young to say. Don't you think it's a little early to write off—pardon the pun—poetry and fiction and journaling?"

"I guess I just know my own limitations," I said self-deprecatingly, winding down our conversation. She was going to be my AP teacher next year, anyway—we'd have more chances to talk then. And I was anxious to get back to the group. They were talking about going to a movie and I didn't want to miss out. They were the closest thing to a clique I had.

All of Ashbury High is divided into three main groups: the rich kids, the jocks, and The Twenty—my nickname for the approximately twenty most overachieving, good-school-bound juniors. They were a social force to be reckoned with, no matter how nerdy. Less important socially (in order) are the partyers, the stoners, the do-gooders, the geeks and freaks.

I was just barely in The Twenty, possibly GPA #19

or 20 itself, but I was in. In the overinflated world of AP

grades and extra credit, staying in the top 10 percent is pretty fricking difficult. But if it wasn't for them, I wouldn't really have had any place in the school hierarchy. I'd be even more of a no one. I sucked at sports, was financially middle class (no matter how upper), never got invited to the good parties, and my interests (making beaded jewelry, e.g.) had no bragging rights among my peers. Nor did they look good on college applications. They were personal. I was personal. Even a little introverted, some might say.

So the people in *Veritas*, the French Club, Model U.N., and everything else were the closest thing I had to a social scene.

"Hey, what are we doing?" I asked, bouncing up to Kevin, the current head of The Twenty. I had thought he was cute for about one marking period, but constant competition doesn't really do much for sexual attraction.

"Oh, I don't know," he sighed, rolling his eyes. "I think we're going to see that action-thriller thing Sonia's cousin is in. Either that or the new Wes Anderson."

Well, that first one sounded kind of exciting. Even if the movie sucked, we would sort of know someone in the credits.

"What are *they* doing here?" someone else asked— GPA #5, as a matter of fact—indicating the door with a similar roll of her eyes.

Lida and Suze, my peeps from the hood and my

oldest friends, had finally shown up. I had invited them along to whatever everyone decided to do after the meeting. We did almost everything together, but somehow didn't come across as the Charlie's Angels trio we should have been.

I was the natural blonde, though it had a hint of red from some Irish somewhere back on my mom's side. Light skin, freckles, blue eyes, pixie nose. Unfortunately, rather than being the *bombshell* blonde, I looked adorable in a baseball cap with a ponytail sticking out the back. Maybe that would change someday when I grew breasts.

Suze was the really beautiful one, theatrical and dark-haired, with very light brown eyes and perfect red lips. HUGE knockers. And she had this aura that made everything she did sparklier and brighter than anything else in the room (I'm immune through long, repeated exposure). She never stopped moving, pouting, posing. Her teeth were very white.

Lida (rhymes with *weed-a*, perfect for her current incarnation as perpetually mellow chronic) had large, wide-set eyes and long black lashes that made her always look sleepy, cool, or sarcastic. Under her lids her irises were a very dark blue. Hers was the only hair that didn't need all kinds of crap to give it volume: large, wavy curls that could look elegant pinned up if she gave a rat's ass and didn't have the thread-wrapped-with-cowrie things going on. She was a little heavier

than Suze and me, but not fat; sort of this Earth Goddess
Mother shape which low-slung jeans and camo pants
always emphasized.

(Dave was also there, an arm around Lida with his
hand in her back pocket. Even Suze and I couldn't tell if
they were actually dating—or if he was just her dealer.
Since he was funny and game for anything, we never
really objected to his presence.)

The three of them . . . didn't really fit in here. Lida
could have been in with the rich kids but opted out for the
stoners. Suze . . . uh . . . Suze liked boys. Which did nothing to increase her popularity as a whole. None of them
was in The Twenty.

But I didn't think it would really matter.

"I invited them," I said, trying not to sound defensive.
"They're cool."

"This was supposed to be a *Veritas*-only thing," Kevin
said, a little nasally. "There's no room in the cars."

"Oh, for Christ's sake, Kevin, do you know how
retarded you sound?" Will said, coming to my rescue. "*I'll*
drive them."

Kevin huffed, "Whatever," while sort of flouncing
away.

"Hey, thanks," I murmured, giving the thumbs-up
to Lida and Suze. Lida thumbed me back. Suze didn't
notice, too busy frowning over a couple of bills in her
hand, making sure she had enough for the movie. Like
many of the wealthier kids in Ashbury, her allowance

was generous—bordering on the unlimited—but restricted to the AmEx card that piggybacked on her dad's so he could see her every expenditure. Cash was a dying commodity among my friends, in some ways more valuable because of the untraceable things they could buy. In Susan's case, cigarettes, birth control pills, and R-rated movies.

"No problem," Will answered back with a smile. He was one of those rare people who managed to remain an individual entity without being relegated to freak status. We'd known each other since kindergarten, before all the social divisions began. His mom was white and his dad was Dominican (I couldn't tell you what that meant when they first moved to Ashbury, but my parents sure could), and he somehow wound up looking like a taller than average Mayan: aquiline nose, blunt proportions, dark hair, clear coffee skin.

"But, could you carry my shit for me?" he asked, indicating his notebook and my bag.

"Of course," I sighed. Everything was a negotiation. Nothing was free.

On the way home, I slumped in the front seat, thinking about the movie.

"I don't think I get it," I finally admitted aloud. "I liked the fish and the weird music, but I don't really get what the point of the whole movie was. I mean, the guy goes to kill the shark that killed his friend, but *doesn't*, and then, like, his son shows up out of nowhere, and *he* dies. . . . Wasn't that kind of random?"

To be fair, I often have trouble getting into a movie, or "suspending my disbelief" for more than a minute at a time. I can never concentrate properly and my thoughts begin to wander. Sometimes I miss entire plot points (ditto for lectures, homework reading, class discussion . . .).

"Wait, what shark?" Suze piped up from the back.

Then again, compared to Suze, I'm like a virtual total-recall.

"The shark he was going to get revenge on for killing his friend," Will explained patiently, both hands on the wheel as we gracefully turned a curve. "The big thing at the end? The whole reason for the expedition?"

"Oh." I could hear the confused pout in her voice. "I sort of missed the end. There was this *really* cute guy from Lewis next to me."

"And you were what, too busy sharing popcorn?" I muttered, just low enough for Will to hear. I had actually considered getting up and going to the bathroom at one point just so I could move seats. Did Suze have to be so *loud* when she flirted?

Will smiled.

Lida gave a distinctly unfeminine snore and turned over in the back next to Suze. She was in the sleepy stage of being stoned, smiling and comfortable and completely oblivious.

"Well, think about what *wasn't* there," Will pointed

out after a moment. "We never saw or heard the editor who got Cate Blanchett pregnant. We never actually saw Steve's friend who died, except in a video flashback. We never saw his dad. And we're told that there's no way he could even have had a son."

"So?" I asked half defensively, half curiously. Who thought about what *wasn't* in a movie?

"So . . . did you notice that no one was upset when Owen Wilson died? It was almost like Steve's son never really existed, he was just a figment of everyone's imagination. So he's like all the others . . . all different aspects of being a father, or the stages of a man's life. The guy who helps conceive a baby, the son, the father figure, the adult friend. The movie was all about how Steve Zissou was trapped as a sort of teen who never wants to grow up. At the end, when he picks up Willem Dafoe's nephew, it shows he's finally matured a little, ready to be more of a father figure."

I thought about what he said. It was hard. The thinking, I mean. But as I walked my way mentally through the movie, it all fit.

I *never* got stuff like that. My essays for English were badly labored attempts at finding subtext and figuring out what the author was *implying*—where all I really found was plot.

Let's face it. I wasn't really Twenty material.

I looked out the window at the woods beyond the pavement. Thinner and thinner every year, as a new strip mall or condo development or whatever went up.

But for now you still couldn't see to the other side; just trees mixing with the dark sky until everything was blurred and black in the distance, no lights puncturing it.

My house was first and I was glad to jump out, still depressed that I had missed the whole point of the movie and sort of embarrassed that Will had done us the favor of driving us home. I slammed the door before Suze or Lida could suggest we hang out afterward, and went around the SUV to the driver's side. Will unrolled the window to talk to me. It was all extremely grown-up. Weird.

"Hey, uh, thanks," I said, trying not to bite my lip, looking him in the eye. I used every possible chance to practice for college interviews, to shed the shy teenager thing in favor of something brighter and more, well, acceptable. I couldn't help playing with my necklace, though, a dangly tasseled, beaded affair, the last one I made before junior year began.

"No problem." He gave a soft smile and rolled his eyes again; he knew just exactly how nice he was for driving all of us. I wish I could have offered something in return, like a latte or a study session. I hate hanging debts. "See you Monday."

The window hummed up, sealing the occupants of the giant space vehicle, and it rumbled off into the night. Our street was one of the older ones, dark, and it felt extremely lonely as they pulled away, like they were stranding me on an empty planet. Once they were gone, silence descended. Not even crickets.

Finally I turned around and went in.

"Thyme!"

The front door opened and my mother's voice hit me at the same time as the blast of brightness and heat from the house, somehow unwelcome even after the black chilliness of the spring night. Oh, and yes, my name is Thyme. As in Parsley, Sage, Rosemary, and. It's the name of an expensive restaurant They used to go to in the city. They joked: After I was born, They couldn't afford to go to a place like that for a long time, and wanted to commemorate it. They also liked to joke that I'm the most beloved mistake in the world. Pretty hilarious parents, no?

"How was the *movie*?"

My mom is one of those people who stays dressed right until bed. Her hair remains as neat and flat as it was in the morning, her makeup retouched if necessary, gold watch, triple strand of pearls, even socks and shoes remain in place until she "turns in for the night." That day she sported a crisp khaki number, desperate for summer, and her blue eyes were fixed on me with that interested brightness you normally associate with birds.

"It sucked." It did. Really. I wasn't trying to be hostile. There just wasn't anything else to say.

"Who was there?"

I really wished she would bless some other teenager

with her interest, someone who was crying out for
parental attention. "davidsuzelidawillkevinsoniameera.
I guess."

"Meera? You don't talk about her much anymore."

"She's a freak, Mom." I threw my jacket over the chair
in the hall that wasn't supposed to be used for that purpose but was nevertheless a shapeless pile of wool and
cotton, and buttons. There might still actually have been
some scarves under there; it had been a while since my
parents' last fight about it.

Final words flung out, I stomped upstairs, shouting a
mental good night to wherever my dad was.

Someone else in my position probably would have
thrown herself onto her bed, grabbed a stuffed ani-
mal or favorite book or whatever, turned up the music,
and stared at the ceiling until falling asleep. Not me. I
pulled off my shoes and jeans and shirt and brought my
WorldCiv textbook and notebook and highlighter under
the covers with me. I was never one of those it-comes-
to-me-easily types—it took all my effort just to be in the
lowest 5 percent of the Twenty. I can guarantee you no
one else who went out to a movie that night, that *Friday*
night, was going back to do homework.

Well, that was the plan.

Unfortunately, fifteen minutes later I was as sound
asleep as my happier, cuddly-monkey-hugging counter-
parts.

2

Jesus of Suburbia

From the bible of "none of the above"
On a steady diet of
Soda pop and Ritalin

                                                     —Green Day

Ah, Saturday mornings. Pancakes for breakfast. The smell of them took me on the short, fast trip from dreaming about something good to wakefulness to realization that I had fallen asleep when I had meant to study. Nine hours had somehow passed. I must have woken up sometime during the night and stumbled to the bathroom to pee and swish some mouthwash around in place of brushing; at that point, however, any thought of actually cracking the books was as ridiculous as the boogie monster who supposedly once lived in the back of my closet.

"Fuck."

But I said it halfheartedly, more like the echo of a real sentiment. I should have gotten a double espresso to go after the movies. Tastes like motor oil, but it would have done the trick. I prepared for my morning role, pulling on my old blue bathrobe and bunny slippers, sprinkling water in my eyes for a quick wakeup (the real cleansing, a three-part ritual involving industrial-strength chemicals, would come later). I stumbled downstairs and on cue my dad turned around, towel over his shoulder, pan full of pancake, bright giant smile on his face, like holy crap, aren't I the best father ever.

"Pancakes for breakfast!"

Um, der. It's only been that way for a billion years now. Mom was sorting through bills and mail with French-manicured nails, making little organized snickety sounds.

And I know for a fact that my dad can cook things other than pancakes. Mom says They used to take turns making dinner. During my tenure in the Gilcrest household I had yet to see him make anything besides pancakes, frozen pizza, and reservations. Cooking was one of those things that I had been vaguely meaning to learn—seemed useful, good to know before I go to college. But on the rare occasions we don't get takeout, Mom cooks *fast*, and complicated. I just want to know how to make a goddamn chicken, not something off of Emeril Lagasse's show.

Whoops, almost forgot my line.

"Yay—*pancakes*."

I slid down into my seat. Dad artfully slipped a pancake off the spatula and onto my plate. Without looking up from my pills, I reached for the syrup—Aunt Jemima, this time. For a family that spends over a hundred bucks a month on cable, you'd think we could afford some of that *real* organic maple syrup that Meera's family uses.

At the upper-right corner of my plate, about two o'clock, was an ugly buff rainbow of vitamins. One long "super C," a nauseating calcium made from oyster shells—the kind you pave driveways with, I think—a clear-gel vitamin E that will explode if you heat it up in your fingers and pop it right, a bright red multivitamin, and an orangish one for teenagers. The last one is the most depressing in some ways. When I was a kid, the pill was equally orangish, but it was chewy and tasted like oranges. The grown-up ones weren't chewable at all and tasted like ass.

But surely people who put out this many pills would be somewhat sympathetic to my cause.

"Um." I cleared my throat. I didn't really want to ruin the Saturday morning forced happiness we all enacted—it was still happiness. Then again, it was also a crock of shit. And I was still depressed about the whole missing-the-point-of-the-movie thing from the night before. "I really think I should be checked out by a doctor."

"Why? Do you have mono?" The nails paused in their walk through ecru envelopes, my mom's already-lipsticked mouth pursed somewhere between an "o" and a "grrr." They're always afraid it's mono. Mom laughs and talks about how she had it as a teenager,

how everyone had it; Dad gets serious, looks at me with
a squint, and starts muttering about school days lost and
how I'll never catch up.

Like I'm caught up now.

"Uh, not that kind of doctor."

"She's talking about ADD again," my dad said, rolling his eyes and carefully pouring more batter into the pan. He has a special ladle just for pancake batter that stands up when you set it down, with a square bottom. "You don't have it. You're a perfectly normal girl."

"It's ADHD," I corrected him, rolling up the pancake on my plate with extreme precision, not looking either one of Them in the eye. "And no, I'm not. Like, last night—I was supposed to come home and study after the movie. But I just fell asleep. I wasn't really tired or anything, but the moment I opened a book, my eyes closed."

"No one does homework after a movie. Not on Friday nights. That's just weird," Mom said, shaking her head over her coffee.

"They do if they want to get into a good college," Dad said, pointing the spatula at me like I was a piece of evidence at a murder trial. "Don't yell at her for that."

"I can't concentrate," I protested, trying to keep my voice even. Parents are far more likely to listen and believe something speculatively scientific if it's said in the soothing, expert monotone of someone on *60 Minutes* or Dr. Sanjay Gupta on CNN.

They weren't buying it.

"You're concentrating on that *pancake* pretty well," my mother pointed out, eyeing my belly and flipping through her mail again.

The nice thing is, I guess, that if I ever do get to go see a shrink, it will be for something easy, like anorexia, and the probable cause will be easy to diagnose.

Once our game of breakfast charades was over, I returned upstairs to really wash and shower.

Oh, all right, that was a little harsh. Look, I love my parents. I really do. I was just beginning to realize I might not . . . *like* everything about Them. In the last few years They had gone from being MOM and DAD with all the good and bad that means to, well, being actual humans. Mom always meant well, but tried too hard and often wound up emotionally flailing out all over the place. Dad was . . . I don't know, colder than even a stereotypical American dad should be. More distant. If things got emotionally messy, he withdrew. Like, he had no problem talking to me about my period when I first got it, but when I started to cry because I didn't want to grow up he clapped me on the shoulder and bought me an MP3 player.

Until I figured out how to deal with the new Them, my usual response was to *stay away*.

So that morning I barricaded myself in my room and decided to start on something easy, because it was Saturday, because I went to the movies the night before, and didn't want to dip right into pre-calc. English was a good choice—we were reading *A Tale of Two Cities*. It

was the best of times, etc., etc. In some ways, it was sort
of a break anyway—I never had time to read just for fun,
just for myself. If I was sick I would borrow one of Mom's
mysteries, but that was about it, and I never finished
them—usually I got better first.

The only thing I could think of while reading was,
Holy shit, life must have sucked back then. Unless you
were the one who got to wear the silk and the crown. And
even then, I suspected that in the next hundred pages or
so, life wouldn't turn out so good for them, either. . . .

I stopped at exactly fifty pages, because—picture me
rocking back and forth autistically—that's the goal I set
for myself. Then it was time for history. But when I dug
into my bag to fish out the giant, stupid, impossible book,
my fingers came across an unexpected texture: not the
slick lenticular covers on my own textbooks, or the rough
papery recycled cardboard feel of my six class note-
books. No, this was thick, with a thick coil cover, alien to
the usual residents of my overloaded bag. I pulled out a
bulky, awkward five-subject über-notebook with a shiny
mottled red cover, filled with the tiny, cramped writing
that was so Will. I forgot to give it back to him at the end of
the night. I flipped through it curiously, looking for some
indication of something: personality, likes, dislikes—how
often do you get to look at the notebook of someone
you're sort of friends with but don't really know?

His notes were extremely more to the point than mine.

There were angular sketches of spaceships that looked like he hadn't lifted the pen off the page once in the making. Also a lot of Mexican-looking things, chubby gods and strange symbols and helmets and angry eyeless men with sharp noses. I wondered if they were Dominican or not, or if native Dominicans even had a culture like the Aztecs or whatever. There was a coffee splotch, dried and dark, which he had drawn over with a blue pen to make it look like our fat guidance counselor, Ms. Bentley. She was sort of Jabba the Hutt style, and he had added a surprisingly good likeness of Kevin Moore on a leash, complete with metal bra and revealing skirt. I actually chuckled.

It was weird—Will and I used to play together after school all the time when we were ten, but I didn't know anything about the guy he'd grown up into. Something happened after elementary school—he went somewhere else for a year or something, rumors abounded—and when he returned, lines had already been drawn between the genders, new groups formed.

This was a tiny glimpse into the him *now*, a cross-section on a slide of what was under the anger and sardonic smile—and I thought I'd probably really like him, if he ever let me in.

If he chose to actually do any homework this weekend—doubtful, he was a first-class slacker—he would need this notebook. And I could definitely use a break in an hour.

The Torreses lived several complexes—excuse me, neigh-
borhoods—away from ours. Ashbury has roads laid out
like wide, squirmy cartoon streets, a board game in gray
and yellow. Another time, years ago maybe, I would
have walked. But driving privileges were still pretty fresh
and Mom's car was new, a big sparkling silver Lexus
thing with more internal gadgets than the space shuttle.
I already knew how to operate them all. Because it was
spring, I didn't need the buttwarmer.

Their house was older and larger than ours. No one
on his street had a pool; instead, there were stone walls,
purely decorative or whose function was to keep the
yard, the old trees, and the inhabitants from touching the
sidewalk below. An old-fashioned, upper-class kind of
street. Even the sky seemed a little darker, probably from
all of the trees, but it felt like just one more touch of age.
Just a few years ago I would have thought: *What a great
street for trick-or-treating.*

No one looked out the kitchen window as I pulled in, or
came to the door before I knocked. Eventually Mrs. Torres
appeared in the doorway, eyes lighting up when she saw
me. It was nice to be the object of that kind of smile.

"Hey, uh, Will left his book in my bag last night, and I
just came over to return it."

"Oh, Thyme, of course. He's up in his room. You remember where it is, right?" She spoke quickly, covering some
fast emotion—a slight lowering of the lids, a whisper of

sadness. Something an adult didn't want a teenager to see.

"Thanks, yeah, no problem."

I made my way past the kitchen and up the stairs, strange smells resettling themselves in my nose as they slowly became remembered. Slightly exotic spices, Clorox, and something that could only be described as the Torres household. Will's mom—or Will's mom's housecleaner—didn't keep her house as spotless as Mom (and Maria) kept ours, but then again, there was a lived-in feel to it that never made you think that any chair or room was off-limits, like the Sitting Room at home. I found myself skipping up the stairs the way I did years ago, old memories confusing themselves with the present.

"Hey." I knocked on his hollow wood door, feeling flushed and slightly exuberant. "Surprise."

Will was sitting on his bed, staring at something in his hand.

"Hey," he said dully. No surprise, no interest, no nothing. I hadn't come over in, like, six years and *this* was his response?

"You, uh, forgot your notebook," I said weakly, waving it.

He shook his head and sighed deeply. "Yeah. Thanks. Come on in."

I came, looking around his room as eagerly as I had flipped through his notes. There was a Mumford & Sons poster and one of something called Lali Puna, *Lord of the Rings*, and another one that looked like *Lord of the Rings* but wasn't, called Zoso. His room was neat but cluttered, everything different since I had last seen it, except for a *Star Wars* mobile in the corner. Excuse me, *model*. There were dozens of other . . . *models* . . . everywhere, as if they had bred quietly and steadily through the years, replicating themselves. Spaceships and dragons and futuristic cars and superheroes and monsters. Each was intricately detailed and flawlessly painted, with shadows in the eyes on the creatures and pings on the ships from interstellar flotsam and jetsam.

Being alone in a room with a guy—even one you're not sure you're attracted to yet—sort of charges the air, makes you notice things you wouldn't normally, take down details of the situation. Like the fact that Will was a tiny bit pudgy, but not in a bad way. I think a lot of it was sort of muscles-in-waiting; he was square and compact like an action figure. He was frowning, making his eyes more slanted, a tiny hint of other worlds in his otherwise very real-and-here personality. Something exotic that had managed to creep in and survive our school system.

"What's going on?" I asked neutrally, sitting on the edge of his bed. He held up the tiny thing he had been staring at, a dark orange bottle with a white lid. My heart skipped when I saw the label: RITALIN. 10 MG.

"My parents have decided that I have 'social adjustment issues,'" he said bitterly. "'I have unmitigated anger.' 'I fail to behave normally.' I rage."

He was talking. To *me*. Delicate steps were required. "Dude," I said as gently as I could, "you did smash Tommy

Halder's mountain bike." It was really expensive—a Gary Fisher. Tommy went to Lewis Prep with all of the other super-rich kids. There was no proof it was Will, but those of us who were pretty sure never ratted him out. Tommy was a dick, and the first—unconvicted—suspect when a couple of horribly mangled squirrels and small dogs were found at the park a few years ago.

Will shrugged with one shoulder.

"He totally had it coming."

I had seen the anger in Will's eyes before, like when someone was talking trash about one of his friends or whatever. It was scary, not cute. Black and bottomless, to the depth of his pupils.

"It's not so bad," I said, shrugging. I wanted to say it was kind of funny, because I had just been begging Mom and Dad to get me to a shrink with the appropriate prescription pad and fast pen, but to him it probably wasn't that funny at all.

Will was a slacker, the sort who is probably smarter than the teacher—smarter than all of us—and mouths off when completely inappropriate. Nor did he have the grades to get by. Personally, I wouldn't have diagnosed ADHD, I would have said bipolar or developmental anger or something. Paxil or Zoloft, not Ritalin.

"They're trying to fucking drug me into submission," he said through clenched teeth, gripping the bottle in a tight fist. "I don't act like all the other drones so they want to medicate me into one."

There's really not much you can say to something like that. Besides, he looked like he wanted to just talk. Get it out.

"It's your sexy, emotional Latino heritage," I joked. "The whities in the counselor's office are terrified of that."

He looked at me for a long moment, and I was terrified that I had just crossed the line.

Then he cracked up.

"You're probably right. Fucking gringos. I'm too much for them." His face relaxed, and so did I, noticing the difference of color between his white teeth and his cheeks. "I'm still not taking these," he said with one last fit of anger across his face, and hurled the bottle of pills into the corner of his room. "You want to go get a café con leche with me, señorita?"

Wow. Almost kind of like a date.

"Uh, if Starfucks makes them, sure."

"Whatever. A latte will do. Let me just go take a whiz and we're out of here."

A weird scene. A strange sudden closeness. It was kind of cool that he trusted me enough to open up like that. Was it just because I was there? Shown up just minutes after what looked like the Big Family Discussion? Or was it because it was *me*, Thyme Gilcrest?

Me, who the moment he was out the door was down on my hands and knees scrabbling for the bottle and then shoving it into my pocket.

3

White Rabbit

One pill makes you larger
And one pill makes you small · · ·
                    —Jefferson Airplane

There's this drug that the military has. No really, this isn't like an urban legend. It's *real*. The air force uses it. Pilots take it and it lets them stay perfectly awake and super focused for, like, three days. Jetfighters can fly around and scan and bomb or whatever for seventy-two hours straight. (And truckers get pulled over for driving on speed or overdoses of NoDoze. Is there no justice?)

I don't know what happens at the end of the three days. I guess they probably collapse. In the best of all worlds they sleep it off for thirty-six hours or so. In reality, I'll bet their systems are probably so weak and exhausted some of them have heart attacks. Disposable soldiers.

Anyway, if it *doesn't* cause heart attacks, why can't the rest of us get some? How great would that be? Three days on of intense concentration and three days off. I'd probably do, like, Friday Saturday Sunday and try to catch up on sleep at lunch or at home or in class Monday Tuesday Wednesday. Unless there was a test Friday, in which case I'd probably take it Wednesday Thursday Friday, or maybe Thursday Friday, to make sure it didn't wear off in the middle of the exam.

Anyway, I set Saturday night aside to try a Ritalin.

Now some people might freak out at the idea of trying a new drug at home by themselves. Even prescription drugs. Have you ever read the "possible side effects" warnings in all the different drug brochures out there? I mean, *really* read them? I'm sure most smart hypochondriacs stop at "fatigue headache dizziness backache fever diarrhea constipation rash and blurriness of vision." But if you can manage it, the second paragraph can list everything from oily farts to all your skin falling off to heart attacks and strokes.

All your skin falling off.

I used to frequent this website for users who would announce what they were doing and then post what happened to them, what they felt. LSD and crack and twelve bottles of NyQuil and whatever. I think a lot of voyeurs were hoping for psychedelic trips or sudden death, but I was really hoping for someone to describe an oily fart or their skin falling off.

But as these brave psychonauts were proving with their own bodies: Nothing ventured is nothing gained.

I took precautions, programming 911 into speed-dial 5 on the phone (it's in the middle of the keypad) and kept a thermometer and a big glass of water nearby. I pretended to work until They left, the little pill set in a position of honor on a brass and velvet pedestal thing that used to support a Ukrainian painted Easter egg (it broke a long time ago). I couldn't stop looking at it.

I mean, it's kind of exactly like an Easter egg.

Approximately the right shape, a pastel shade. Only the surprise isn't finding the egg, it's what the egg gives you, like a random powerup in a videogame.

Ah, I shouldn't be so melodramatic. I had a pretty good idea of what was going to happen—other people without ADHD scored Ritalin all the time at school, and it's all over the Internet.

But isn't the concept of *drugs* in general kind of cool? I mean, the right ones, not illegal ones. They can't make you fly, but they can make you feel like you do. They can make you jump higher and run faster. Think better and smarter. Make your cough and cold go away. Put you to sleep. Wake you up. Get old geezers' johnnies going and put the kibosh on sexual predators. They can grow more hair for you or stop it from growing on your chin. They can give you clear, beautiful skin. They can keep you from getting pregnant or help you to *get* pregnant. Cure your salmonella, your gonorrhea, your fricking foot fungus. Forget just uppers and downers: Prescription drugs really are the magic potions of the real world.

As soon as the door slammed and They were gone for the night, I took my hands off the keyboard—uh, I was actually just surfing plots of upcoming shows on the CW—and slowly, without rushing it, picked up my glass of water and my Ritalin. I felt like I should say something, do a little ritual, because if this worked right, it would be the end of all of my high school problems.

"Over the lips and past the gums . . . ," I said, unable to think of anything else, and popped it. I took a long drink of water and forced myself to slowly finish the whole glass. Dehydration is a common side effect for a lot of drugs, and I wanted some cushion in my belly so I wouldn't vomit it up instantly if things went that way. Probably should have taken it with milk or a piece of bread instead.

I opened my WorldCiv textbook, uncapped my highlighter, and started a new document on my computer—to take notes on anything I might be feeling. I password-protected it immediately.

```
May 12 Tuesday 7:59 R trials 10 mg
```

I even wrote down the date and time—yeah, anal, but you never know how a drug's going to affect you at different times. Like my mom gets wasted on a single glass of wine the first day of her period. Suze is like that too. She always makes a joke about going for a drink after "giving blood"—her brother in college actually does that; it's a cheaper drunk.

8:05

Nothing.

8:10

I sneezed. I considered writing that down, but then realized it was probably stupid and had nothing to do with the Ritalin.

8:15

Antsy and bored, I started glancing over the pages on the Russian Revolution. The one photograph was really pretty: black-and-white of some straight-backed aristocrats, not dressed like you think of kings and queens and counts and things should be, but the boys in almost military clothes and the girls in beautiful tight-fitting gowns with big rings and furs. Yeah, I know, bad furs. But somehow it's easier to forgive when the coats are that gorgeous and the people who wear them live in a crappy cold place like Russia.

8:26

I suddenly realized I had been staring at the photo like I was high for several minutes. I did a quick mental check, looking around the room and standing up and sitting down, but it definitely wasn't like drinking or pot. No wooziness. It felt more like when you have *just enough* caffeine—not enough to make you shaky, just enough so that you feel razor-sharp and witty, and the world has clean, optimistic, bright edges to it.

Unlike caffeine, I didn't jump from one thought to another, or have any weird creative moments or start pacing or anything.

I started to actually *read* about the Russian Revolution . . .

. . . and at one o'clock, when They finally came home, I was still reading.

4

Ritalin 202

Romanov, Karenina, Bolsheviks.

1912, dude with the crazy long schlong, proletariat.

D, Lenin.

The answers were coming to me as fast as I wrote.

Usually I don't study well or efficiently—but under My New Influence I was able to read, re-read, and read again the textbook, my notes, and occasional online help (which is where the trivia about Rasputin's studly junk came from), so it sunk in despite my stupid self.

I had to pause once to shift in my seat, turning so my straight-as-spit hair fell in a strawberry blond water-fall that sort of accidentally blocked Suze's view of my paper. This wasn't done in competition—she's not even on the waiting list for The Twenty. No, this was simple annoyance; I had grown tired of her not-studying routine about three years back. She shouldn't even be in the accelerated class; of the two of them, Lida was the more qualified—but she was stoned when we took the placement exams and Suze's mom bitched about her getting put in the B-levels.

I had to switch my tactics every once in a while so she didn't get too suspicious. Next time maybe I'd let her see my answers, if I was feeling generous.

The part where I really slowed down was the essays. At first I was a little shocked, 'cause I thought my New Brainy Superpowers would make the whole test a breeze. But I'll be the first to admit that drugs don't really make you brilliant. Like caffeine may make you see connections faster than you did before, but serious thought still required high-functioning brain matter.

Compare and contrast the Russian Revolution with the French Revolution.

All I could think of was stinky, oppressed peasants and their respective foods: crepes and blinis. Let them eat borscht.

Who do you think was more pivotal to the Revolution, Marx or Lenin?

Please see above, re: millions of pissed-off, disaffected peasants. Or, None of the Above; see Smith & Wesson.

Do you think the Romanovs deserved their fates? Use specific historic examples to back up your opinion.

Ah. This was one I could sink my teeth into: the bullshittiest of them all.

I was one of the first ten people to hand the test back, quite a surprise for anyone who cared (okay, just Suze and me). Usually I'm gripping my pen in white-knuckled hands until the very last second, going over and over my answers until the paper is forcibly taken from me. When I was in elementary school, they were going to put me with the retarded—excuse me, *special*—kids, because I failed every timed math test. My parents got seriously involved in that battle. It turned out that every answer I managed to finish was *right*—I just freaked out and did them very slowly and rechecked each one a thousand times, so I never made it more than halfway through the test.

The bell rang and Suze groaned, pulled herself out of her chair, flung her test at the teacher's desk—Ms. Hendel gave a tight-lipped look of disapproval—and swung herself into place next to me.

"That *sucked*," she announced dramatically, looking out the corner of her eye to see if Dave noticed. He was one of the current grove of trees she was barking up. Awkward because of his, uh, relationship with Lida. But the stoner seemed impervious to Suze's advances—very strange. Usually, no one was.

I shrugged.

"Man, you were fast on that one," she added, reluctantly turning back to me.

"I'm having an up day," I said with a smirk.

"What?" She caught the tone in my voice, gave me a look. I shook my head very slightly and she made the thumb-pinky *phone me later* sign. We were in a crowd, and you could never be too careful. I wasn't even sure how much I wanted to tell her.

Meera tried to slink by. She was staring at the ground or somewhere ahead of her in the middle distance, almost like she was trying to do that thing little kids and bunnies do, hoping they won't get noticed. Frankly, she didn't really need to do that; besides the neither-here-nor-there brown hair color and cut, she dressed like a wallflower: always the same oversize jeans, oversize T-shirt with some tv show or science fiction thing on it. She was taller than all of us, but hunched like it hurt.

I wasn't feeling charitable, so I let her go.

"Hey." (The) Sonia Lansing bounced up to me. She was in The Twenty's top three, a solid contender for valedic- or salutatorian. I could only dream of such GPAs. Freshman year was sort of a wash for me as I got used to the rigors of high school scholarship. She dove in kicking.

Sonia *looked* like someone you would want to give a speech to your class—or sell car insurance. Straight black hair, cute face with serious eyes. At one time she was perfectly proportioned, too, but the eating disorder had taken a toll on her breasts, shoulders, and ass.

Dressed preppie, sucked up to adults like she was a born buttsnorkeler.

"I'm having a party on Saturday, to celebrate the end of the semester. We're going to set up the grill and everything." "We" was her and—I kid you not—our star quarterback and hockey player. Yes, the academic cheerleader was dating the quarterback. Doesn't it just make you sick?

"Sounds like fun," I said politely. And compared to a night at home with Them and a video, it was.

"Bring a six-pack or six cans of produce for the local shelter."

She turned even social occasions into social work.

"Oh, and vegetables or whatever you want to grill."

"Thanks, I will."

"Great! Suze, you can come too. And you can bring Lida, if you want."

She gave me a little shit-eating grin, sort of waved, and spun off.

"How old are we?" I demanded as soon as she was out of earshot. "Forty? *Barbecue in the backyard?*"

"Hey, it's a party, don't knock it," Suze suggested, shrugging. Her one saving grace—I mean, besides being beautiful—was an unflappably optimistic outlook on everything. Yes, annoying at times, but genuine.

Lida dissolved out of the crowd and fell into step with us like we had planned it, like out of a movie, *Ocean's Eleven* or something; and I won't say it was entirely

unrehearsed. The trick is to not look like you're trying, to
not look for your friends' faces in the crowd.

"Hey," Lida said flatly, patting herself all over, looking
for smokes. "I gotta take five—can I bum one?"

Suze obligingly dug through her teddy-bear-dangle-
decorated bag and produced a pack, tipping one out
with the careful practice of someone who can't afford
that many (the cash thing, remember?). One time when
they were giving them out free at this club in the city, she
charmed *three* packs out of the guy—and two were still
in the fridge, hidden behind the crisper.

I kept clenching and unclenching my fists, trying to drop
the phantom pen that still seemed to be clutched there. It
was kind of an anticlimax; I hadn't thought about anything
else that week except for this test, and now it was over.

"But why don't we ever get invited to the *cool* parties?" I whined, already ungrateful for the one party
thrown kindly my way by the gods. Across the hall a pair
of the bigger partyers were laughing and dishing about
some shindig. In a very straight-guy way, with a lot of
hand slapping and expletives.

Lida swung her head slowly around to look at me as if
she were seeing me for the first time. Since it was a Monday
morning, I assumed that it wasn't because she was stoned;
she just probably wasn't wearing her contacts.

"I didn't know you were so interested. In *those* people."

"We're almost *seniors*, for Christ's sake," I pointed out,
a little defensively. "It's been four years and we still don't

get to go to the swinging-from-the-chandeliers champagne parties. I don't want it all the time. I just want the option."

Is that such a surprise? Even us sort-of-introverts want to have fun. I lived in a town *full* of the beautiful people you read about in the gossip pages. I just wanted to be one, once in a while.

Or, you know, at least be *near* one.

"But you'll take us to Sonia's, right?" Suze asked, continuing to fumble around in her purse.

"Yeah, yeah."

I saw Will at his locker—or rather, some empty senior locker that he had taken for his own. Only upperclassmen got ones in the main hall—terribly inconvenient for the rest of us. A funny light went off in my head. Not a big one, not like an idea or a revelation, but a small one, like an LED on a computer that says the hard drive is working or something's up. Like: Huh, you know what? He's almost sort of cute. I hadn't thought of him that way since kindergarten.

Suze pulled out a tiny Nalgene waterbottle—more like a baby bottle, really; I think it even had a key ring on it—and headed for the closest fountain.

"Dry mouth," she explained, making a little motion with her hand like she was a sixty-year-old yenta.

Suze's current prescriptions were Celexa and Wellbutrin. Both were antidepressants; the Wellbutrin counteracts some of the crappier downsides of Celexa and vice versa (even if *she* didn't read her prescription

inserts, I did. As you might have guessed, I find that stuff
fascinating). Dry-mouth and dizziness were only two of
her current problems, but definitely the least annoying.
She also sometimes got dizzy spells; it was like watching
a swan or ballerina slowly collapse. All dick-encum-
bered humans within a twenty-foot radius would leap to
her rescue.

"Man, she should really get off that shit. It fucks with
your whole system," Lida observed.

"Yeah," I muttered before splitting off, our trio dissolv-
ing as easily as it had formed in the swampy biomass of
the school hallways. "*That* really fucks with your system."

Please understand: While not a toker myself, I have
nothing against marijuana. It's *stoners* I can't stand.

"Hey," I said to Will.

"Oh, hey." He looked a little surprised to see me
addressing him directly—like I said, we weren't close
friends. His face was blank, impassive, one eyebrow
raised. Was my motive for approaching him selfless, or did
I feel some guilt over bogarting his pills?

Carefully . . .

"You okay?" I asked.

"Uh, yeah," he said slowly, closing his locker and
spinning the lock. "Thanks. Thanks for . . . letting me vent
the other day."

"No problem," I said with a shrug and a half smile.

"Yeah." He looked down at the ground, frowning, as
if looking there for something else to say. But there were

only dirty tiles and a gum wrapper. "I'm just not going to take them. If they want me to see a therapist, fine, whatever. But I'm really not going to medicate myself into a zombie."

He looked up into my eyes, searching for maybe confirmation or denial, agreement or chastisement.

"You don't have ADHD," I said, rolling my eyes.

"No *shit*," he added with a slight punch to the locker next to his. "I can concentrate just fine when it's something interesting. Just not a lot of this bullshit." He gestured at the halls. I hadn't really thought about it before, but all of the little models he painted didn't paint themselves. Some of them probably took hours.

I felt a flash of annoyance: If he could concentrate long enough to finish putting all the scales on a dragon—complete with damage and rust and pimples or scale-rot or whatever it is that dragons can get—how could he screw up school so badly? If I had *half* of his ability, I wouldn't have needed to steal his meds.

"Oh my God, get this," he said before turning to go, "someone actually offered me twenty bucks for my bottle of Ritalin. Can you believe that? I don't even know where it went. I should look for it."

Shocking.

Especially since everyone knows they go for at least five dollars a pill.

5

This Is a Call

Ritalin is easy
Ritalin is good . . .

　　　　　　　　　–Foo Fighters

"Good work, Ms. Gilcrest. You really seem to be pulling it together."

I was all ready to preen, but the pop quiz Applegate handed back only had a thick-penned "83" at the top.

Turns out Ritalin didn't work so good on math.

Like I said, I know Ritalin doesn't actually turn you into a genius. I'm the student who complains that she understands the concepts but just can't apply them—to which science and math teachers always retort, *well, that means you don't really understand them.*

On Vitamin R, I could study till the cows came home, forcing the shit down until my mind had no choice but to regurgitate it perfectly (instead of getting frustrated, crying, breaking my pencil, eating a pint of ice cream, and then going online to see if there were any new bead projects posted on craftster.org). I could also see similarities between problems on the test and ones from homework assignments. I could take bits and pieces from here and there and make them work, like creating an outfit out of a closet of dirty, ill-fitting clothes.

But that didn't mean I understood it. The points off were for problems I hadn't seen before. Same old Thyme Version 1.0.

There was some good news the next week, though. We got our WorldCiv exams back—half our grade for that marking period, did I mention that?—and I got a big-ass, spanking A.

So, that was basically it for WorldCiv. Second-semester junior year is supposedly the most important for grades, the last ones that colleges really look at. I hear that's not as true anymore, that they also look at first *and* second marking periods of your senior year as well. But . . . still. I could check off this class: done. I'd have to *really* screw up to get below an A. I rock at projects, and with my new special helper, I could work on papers for as long as it takes.

It would have been an A+ except for the essay question, of course. Knowledge can never be replaced by *funny*: My point was merely that if, like the Romanovs, you flaunt not just *jewelry* in front of the masses, but hideously tacky, David Yurman–style jewelry, hey, you were going to get lynched.

"Whoa, kick ass," Suze said, seeing my little victory dance (it involved a lot of arm pumping). She got a C. "Man, I suck."

Meera took hers from the teacher and put it directly into her bag.

"Hey, how'd you do?" I was expansive with relief and freedom.

She shrugged, tucking one of many pieces of flyaway hair behind her ear. "Uh, A. Plus."

"Grind," Suze muttered. Upbeat she may be, but also becoming noticeably unkind to the unbeautiful.

"I didn't study," Meera protested, only making it worse for herself. I felt less hate than wonder, more curiosity than the usual desire to destroy those who float along so effortlessly.

"You must be some kind of freaking genius," I said, sighing.

Meera shrugged again. "I just do the readings. It just sort of makes sense. The things that happened in England and France kind of led to what happened in Russia, in their own way. It's like the whole world was ripe for change."

Now, that was weird. You can't understand history the way you can understand physics and math. Can you? Did she really "get" mass human motivation at the turn of the century?

Suze rolled her eyes.

"Come on." She took my arm—very European, very

hip—and dragged me away. "I need to get out of here, and you need to celebrate."

Meera stood there a moment and then wandered away—somewhat glumly, it looked like. Maybe she was hoping to get asked along to wherever we were going. I felt bad, but she didn't make it easy on herself. Meera never knew how to talk to people or how to make them like her.

But I couldn't help thinking, if just for a second: Maybe, instead of studying by myself or with Suze and Lida, I should try it with her.

Maybe I'd actually learn something.

Overheard near the seniors' lockers:

"No, man, I can't party tonight—I have to be back home later when my grandparents come in. Sober."

"So take a freaking Adderall. Take two before the party."

"What, the study drug?"

"Yeah, it'll totally keep you from passing out. My sister in college does it all the time."

"Dude, I said sober. 'Not passed out' isn't exactly the same thing."

Mom and Dad were so thrilled with my exam that They took a moment out of their evening to talk to me about it.

"A, huh?" my dad said with that sly glance. "Couldn't get an A plus? Huh?" he punched me on the shoulder, ha-ha, old joke. Only it wasn't really a joke if you said it every time, was it? He carefully flipped through to see what I got wrong or what bonus questions I didn't answer.

"That's great, honey, that'll really improve your GPA," my mom said with genuine feeling, taking the exam from him and tapping the A as if to see if it was real. She snicked in her heels into the kitchen, probably to hang it under the memopad shaped like a 40 which Dad got for his last birthday.

I waited for part two of the joke, my eyes squinched shut. It was delayed as Dad popped a vitamin from his Mega Mex Super Cuts Supplement Bastards bottle— the ones that cost sixty bucks for a month's supply. Still, cheaper than Ritalin, huh?

"Gonna make your dad proud, right? Like your cousin Hauser? Gonna give him a run for his money?"

My cousin brings to mind everything you think of when you think of Harvard. He's wealthy, goes to Lewis Prep, wears khaki shorts and scarves in the fall, knows how to sail, and already knew which secret society he wanted to be tapped for. And at the end of those four years the top companies would be lining up to recruit him.

Pigs would fly before Harvard let *my* sorry ass in.

Great jobs only come from going to a good school. Getting into a good school means getting good grades. Like this exam. Which is good. But it also means getting a good score on the SATs, which I hadn't even begun to think about yet. Shit, I needed to sign up for that Kaplan information seminar. Hope there's still space. . . . Otherwise, how would I get a corner office?

End of my junior year was rapidly telescoping into my thirties, and the rest of my life.

Without thinking about it, I put my hand to my chest where my heart had begun to beat out of control. It probably looked really Victorian or something, like I was a woman with the vapors, about to faint.

"You okay?" Dad asked, bending down and lacing his new running shoes.

"Just a little panic attack," I admitted. I wasn't normally afflicted with them—*other* people were, keeling over in gym or the hall, their anorexic little bodies pushed to the limit by worry or study or life or drugs.

Drugs. Hmmm. I'll bet this was a side effect of the Ritalin.

"You should run with me," Dad suggested, standing up and flexing up and down in his shoes. "It would be good for you. Calm your nerves."

"No thanks. Homework calls." And maybe something to eat. As corny as it might have been, a warm glass of milk sounded really good and calming.

"Well, another time maybe." He put his hands behind his head and flexed some more. I guess my dad's good-looking; he's got that perfect runner's body, not too muscled. Strong, trustworthy chin, equally trustworthy full head of thick brown hair. But there was something a little sharp about his features, like he was never completely at rest, always looking to the next thing.

"I've got a race on Saturday, if you want to come and watch," he added. "A 10K."

"For charity or something?"

"No. Wait, yes. *No*. No, just something sponsored by Nike."

He gave me a little salute like I was his captain, already pumping his legs, and was out the door into the warm spring night.

Papa was a rolling stone . . .

"Hey, honey, did you stop by the pharmacy today—oh." Mom came into the room and must have figured out from the cracked door and the lingering scent of something blue and masculine and fresh that her husband had run off. "Shoot. Monica's going on a trip on Thursday and I owe."

She plopped down on the couch. Her light red hair, touched up and grayless, fell gracefully around her head and the back of the couch. In the gloom of the dead sunset she was almost noir, like she could pull a cigarette out of a case and light it, speaking in cryptic phrases about someone dead.

Mom picked at a pillow instead.

"What do you owe?" I asked, breaking the moment. It was too terrible to see her like a character after the camera has moved on.

"Oh, you know, the Xanax pool," she said with a little laugh, nervous because she was talking about Drugs in front of her Teenage Daughter. "At work. Everyone contributes so that when someone has to fly, there's always a few around."

"How . . . Communist," I said. "Contributing to a shared resource, then taking as needed. We just studied it in WorldCiv. 'From each according to his ability, to each according to his need.'"

Imagine, sharing shit like Xanax. Adults had it made. *My* friends—like Sonia—sometimes had to pay ten bucks a pill to that guy who hung out near the pizza place.

"Oh, that's just silly," she said with a wave of her hand. Then she stretched out her foot and slipped off a pump, checking out her pedicure, her calf, a funny bump on her knee.

"What was your favorite subject in high school?" I suddenly asked. I don't know why. In the weird half-light I felt like I could get Mom to answer anything, and yet *this* was the thing that interested me.

She cocked her head like the way her mother, my grandmother, did and bit the end of her thumb.

"History, I guess."

Not the answer I was expecting. What was my favorite class? Well, now that I had an A in it, history, I guess. Twenty years from now would I forget what we were taught in my favorite class too?

I felt my heart flutter again.

Then the moment was over. Mom got up and brushed invisible dust off her skirt.

"Hey, let's go through your closet and get rid of some stuff. I *know* there's clothing in there you've outgrown or don't wear anymore. We can make a big bag and bring it to the Salvation Army."

I walked behind her extra quick, trying to work the extra heartbeat out with forced physical activity. Maybe Dad was right—maybe I *should* go running with him. If I had time.

It was bleak and comforting at the same time. There was this test I had basically taken *pills* to get through, and in twenty years—assuming I got into a good school—it wouldn't matter: The grade remained, the content goes away. I resolved to remember those words, *from each according to his ability, to each according to his need*, to repeat them over and over in my head so I would always remember them, just so it wasn't all a waste.

As we passed the fridge I remembered about the warm milk.

Pity about the Xanax, though; that would have worked a *lot* better.

6

Too Drunk to Fuck

I drank 16 beers
And I started up a fight . . .
                    -Dead Kennedys

On Saturday, Dad came in somewhere between tenth and twentieth. Twelfth, I think. I hung back, embarrassed, as Mom comforted him and he *loudly* went over everything that was wrong with him, with the day, with the track, with his mood, with his shoes. Not enough vitamins. But he gradually brightened the closer we got to the IHOP—hey, it was still a Saturday—and by the time I got my pecan special he was spouting off platitudes like the posterchild of Team Strategizing that he was.

It was all easily bearable because (A): I had pancakes made *by a professional*, and (B): I was going to a party that night. Friends and beer and nothing else to think about.

I had Mom drop me off at the Galleria with the

promise of two hundred bucks for new clothes to make
up for the two bagfuls we got rid of the night before.
Not a ransom, but enough for some spring shit at H&M.
Suze met me there. If you're doing something mindless
and silly, she's your woman, squealing over seven-day
undie packs with monkeys on the butt or encouraging
the Benefit woman to run rampage over your face with
makeup you're not sure you want.

Lida (never a big shopper) came over later, somehow managing to slip past Mom and Dad without
revealing her red eyes or stoned state. She lay on
my bed in her camo pants and ripped Bastille tee
and stared quietly at the ceiling while Suze and I got
ready.

There was definitely a spring *something* in the air.
You know that feeling you get when you're getting
ready to go out and you're suddenly excited for no reason? Like, you have this feeling that something *great* or
mysterious or *romantic* or at least *interesting* is going
to happen? Even though you *know* it's the same stupid
party or movie or dance with the same stupid people—
no tall dark stranger, someone's hot cousin, or frigging
vampire is going to come out of the woodwork to take
you away—you just breathe in that weird, damp-like-
dirt air and feel like it's going to be different this time.
Like a really good song makes you feel, or at the end of
a really good action movie.

I spent hours getting ready, trying on different outfits,

enduring and occasionally listening to comments from the peanut gallery.

"Makes your butt look big."

"Too trashy."

"Too conservative."

"Maybe with a cardigan?"

"Dude, you should totally make *mobiles*."

That was Lida, playing with one of my half-completed glass bead necklaces, staring at All the Pretty Sparklies. Who knows, maybe she was right. Maybe there was a market for expensive trinkets for rich kid stoners to play with.

I finally wound up with pants I already owned, some new bangles, and a new camisole.

And the carefully retouched Benefit.

I didn't notice my hands shaking at first; I always have a little trouble with eyeliner if I'm listening to fast music or am excited about a party. Unfortunately, this time the excitement quickly became another heart-racy attack. Lida noticed immediately when I sat down, face flushed, and she kindly offered to give me a one-hit (she knew I didn't toke, but it was all she had to offer). I shook my head and held my hand up. Suze dramatically got me a glass of water and told me to breathe into a pillow.

"No wait," she added quickly, "that'll smudge your face."

Instead she gave me one of those tiny airplane bottles of vodka she kept stashed in her purse. *That* worked.

"Thanks." After a moment I was breathing normally again. It was only like an ounce of alcohol, but it spread warmly down my throat and calmed my belly.

"No problem. My parents used to give me a tablespoon of brandy whenever I had panic attacks," she said, finishing the rest herself. "It totally works."

Lida snorted. "Remember that time you panicked at Genevieve's sleepover?"

I couldn't help laughing. "Going through their liquor cabinet . . . looking for Courvoisier Cognac VSOP!"

"That's what they always used," Suze said stubbornly. "I thought that's what it had to be to work. Like medicine."

"'Like medicine.' That's awesome," Lida said, still snickering.

"Good medicine," Suze said, toasting her with the empty bottle. It was moments like this that I really remembered why we were all still friends. It wasn't just the shared memories, but how well we still clicked. Even if it was rarer than it used to be. I could see us doing this over a pitcher of martinis someday, in some swank restaurant where we ogled the waiters, or somebody's summerhouse on a girls' weekend away from our husbands.

Feeling better and boosted with a little help from the booze, we drove over—me, because I'd had the least; we weren't total idiots—and walked up to the house like the Three Musketeers with our spurs on (oh, whatever), ready for action and an evening of fun.

"Hey, guys," Sonia said, wearing what must have been one of her "dress up" polos. "You didn't bring any tempeh, did you?"

An hour later I was reclining on an aluminum lawn chair, tipping a beer back and trying to enjoy myself. Lida and Suze were gone, off drinking or chatting. People-watching was dull: Members of The Twenty stood around clusters of sputtering tiki torches, pretending to enjoy their beers, discussing their early SAT scores, and watching other people out of the corner of their eyes. Inside, a bunch of guys were playing videogames. If Meera had been invited, she probably would have been with them.

How could a party like this possibly suck? With the beer and the tiki and the grill?

Well, what makes any party great?

The people.

These people . . . my friends . . . were being kind of boring. And annoying. Why on earth would I want to talk about test scores on a weekend night? I competed with them 24/7 Monday through Friday. And they were *still* competing.

That's why I was sitting by myself, in the corner of the yard.

"This blows," Dave said, stopping by my chair and grinding a cigarette out on the lawn. Suddenly I wished I could be like him.

Lame, huh? "If only I were half as cool as the class's
fucking stoner."

"Where you going?" I asked, faintly hoping it was a
cooler party he would ask me along to.

"Dorianne's actually got a gig at Beanhead's. I guess
I'll go support her."

I couldn't decide whether to laugh or be impressed—
he was ditching free beer and Lida to see a band that
was somewhere between goth and, uh, whatever's
whinier and more modern than goth.

"You want to come?"

Surprisingly nice of him to offer. In my buzzed state
I felt very international, reaching out to all of the tiny
weird nation-states, the stoners and the Beneluxes.

But it was a simple equation: Free beer, plus possibility of more free beer, is greater than or equal to
coffeeshop-with-cover and possibility of having to talk to
Dorianne afterward. I pointed to my half empty bottle in
explanation.

Dave nodded, understanding completely.

Then he took out an Altoids tin—the kind my grandmother used to hold a tiny sewing kit—and opened it,
revealing three joints nestled snugly within like shotgun
shells. After some hemming and frowning and hawing
he picked one and began the elaborate process of prep-
ping it for the journey over.

"I hear you aced that WorldCiv test. You and all
the other monkeys." He jerked his thumb back at the

barbecue, where various Twenty-ites were giggling and squealing about something. "I have to get a fucking A for the rest of the quarter or my old man's gonna *kill* me."

"You need a magic bullet," I said dreamily, thinking of my secret weapon, and then suddenly realized I was using all small-arms metaphors. Ritalin sort of does that sometimes—makes you see connections where there aren't any. You jump from one thing to another, looking for the next.

"Yeah?" he said skeptically.

"Yeah," I said, taking a couple pills out of my purse. Yeah, I know. I was feeling cool just hanging, talking with the stoner. And maybe he was a little cute. "Try these."

"What the fuck are those?" he demanded, leaning over.

"Study aids," I said mysteriously.

"Yeah?" He picked one up and frowned at it.

"Take two," I suggested. "They're small."

"I'm uncomfortable with how our positions have reversed, Gilcrest," he said loudly, but taking the other one, putting both carefully in his tin. "*I'm* the dealer. You're the fucking grade jockey."

I shrugged luxuriously. I couldn't stop thinking about his Altoids tin. I should get one and bling it up. Pimp-o-mints. Heh, heh. That would be sweet.

"Here," he said, tossing me a small joint. I mean, *really* small. It almost looked like those little bangers,

tissue paper wrapped around gunpowder that broth-
ers and nine-year-olds throw at your feet and explode.
"Peace out, you fucking pusher."

I settled back into the chair. I don't do pot. It's just one
of those things I don't do. Drinking is as crazy as this little
"grade jockey" gets. Still, it was kind of neat to *own* a
joint. You never know when it might come in handy. And
there was sort of a coolness factor: Lame party it might
have been, but I was already buzzed, had half a beer in
my left hand and a joint in the other. All free, less the cost
of a few pounds of grilling veggies. Even if I wasn't much
of a toker or a drunk, life was looking pretty good.

And this is where real life diverges from *The Vampire
Diaries* or whatever nighttime show about teens you like.

One of the mega-partyers dropped by with half a
keg (leftover from *his* party, I guess. One of the cool parties, like the ones Lida, Suze, and I were never invited
to. What were they serving there? Imports in bottles?). I
guess Sonia was tutoring him in math or something and
he owed her. His personality alone turned it into a sparkly party for a few minutes. Then he left and took the
interesting with him, and the beer and beer and more
beer turned everyone else into slightly more horny
and outgoing class presidents and yearbook editors.
When Kevin came over and perched on my lawn chair
I decided it was time to leave.

Besides, I had a scant hour to make it home before

my curfew, which had to include time to drop off my two friends.

It was easy to find Lida: I just followed the smoke signals. But it took a lot longer for the two of us to track down Suze in a small study upstairs under our star soccer player—and liplocked like there was no oxygen in the room.

He had a tight kung-fu grip on her left shoulder.

Was he pinning her down? Or keeping her from rolling away?

We'll never know.

When they talk to you about date rape in health class and how alcohol lowers your inhibitions, they never mention what happens when two drunken idiots decide to go at it. Is it rape? Or is there some other legal word?

"Hey," Suze said with a slow, wide smile. Then she pointed to the top of a bookshelf. "Did you see Sonia's mom's collection of Lladró? They're *beautiful*."

I looked up; hundreds of creepy little pastel statuettes stared down at us.

Lida started laughing, but a little ember of something glowed redly in my stomach. It fed itself on the alcohol I had drunk, growing larger and burnier as I became more sober. This wasn't the first time I had—we had—rescued Suze from the result of überdrinking.

I pulled the boy off of her, but Lida had to keep pushing him out of the way; he was so drunk he could barely move. Suze was so drunk she barely noticed.

Her clothing was a mess—I'd say he'd made it to at least third base—but putting her back together wasn't half as hard a trick as getting her home and into bed without her dad smelling or talking to her. Lida and I giggled a lot—it was easy for Lida—and sort of kept Suze between us, rushing her along and upstairs as if we were full of Teenage Girl Hysterics. Mr. Merritt was a single dad and easily charmed, but nasty as a pitbull when it came to illicit substances in the hands of the underage.

But like I said, this wasn't the first time we had done this.

As Suze lay semi–passed out in bed, face all innocent and relaxed, I had this weird, sudden urge to punch her in the face. Over and over and over again.

It was two by the time I got home, two hours past curfew. I was so exhausted and fed up that if Mom and Dad caught me and yelled at me, I decided I would just tell them the fucking truth. Let them talk to Suze's dad. Maybe it wouldn't be such a bad idea for her to get caught.

But They were still out and I had the house, the fridge, and the *big* bathtub to myself. By two thirty I was in bed, washed clean of the night, not thinking about how stupid I was, Suze was, Lida was, *everyone* was.

At four a.m. I was wide awake, gluing everything sparkly I could find in my beading supplies to an old Altoids tin I found in the back of the kitchen cabinets. And, as a lark, I also prettied up the bottle of Ritalin.

At seven forty-five I was done.

At noon, Mom woke me up with a shake and a wry comment:

"I guess it's true what doctors say—teenagers really do sleep all the time."

7

Mother's Little Helper

There's a little yellow pill. . . .
And it helps her on her way,
   gets her through her busy day . . .
                    -Rolling Stones

Monday I sort of kept an eye out for Will—thinking about him was like a little bright thing in my head. I finally caught up with him at the end of the day, when he was getting ready to go home, standing by the smokers' door.

"Hey," I said as casually as I could.

"Gilcrest." He pulled surprisingly black earphones and wires out of his head—almost everyone who listened to music in our class grew the white tentacles; they were iPodpeople who didn't look anything like the cartoon ads. Another point for Will, something I had never noticed before.

I put on my best flirt smile. "Didn't see you at the party Saturday night."

"Which one?"

That stopped me. It would never have occurred to me in a million years that Will would be invited to one of the big parties; besides the occasional ferocious temper, he was famous for pretty much doing his own thing. Then again, I guess that could sort of make him attractive to both genders; the guys who *want* to be macho and independent but are really just all talk.

"Doesn't matter," he added. "Didn't go to either."

Aha. My first guess was right.

But he didn't give any clue as to what he'd actually been doing. And there was no way to guess; his brown eyes were unblinking and fathomless.

The conversation could have gone anywhere from there. I was kind of interested to see where it would end up.

But the next thing I knew there was a hand on my shoulder and I was being spun around, smacked face-to-face-to-face with Lida and Suze. Lida was the one with the punishing grip; Suze just pouted.

"Dude, we totally tried to call you all day yesterday," Lida said. "Where were you?"

I tried to turn back, to at least say good-bye, but Will had put his earphones back in, not upset, not annoyed, just continuing on with his life since it was obvious our conversation was over.

Sunday I was irritable all day. Like, asshole irritable. I barely spoke to Mom and Dad and refused to answer the phone when Suze and Lida called. I'd spent all Saturday

with them—wasn't that enough? Just thinking about Suze
made me angry, and I was tired of trying to talk to Lida
when she was stoned. It was boring.

"I was still sick from Saturday night." Not a total lie—I
was sick of everyone.

Lida raised an eyebrow. "You barely had anything.
Suze here is the one who should still be in bed."

Suze gave a glamorous smile, then tilted her head
back and dropped some Visine into her eyes.

Der. Like I could actually fool the two people here
who had known me the longest. I mean, that's one of the
great and horrible things about old friends—they keep
you honest. When nothing else can.

"I just wanted to talk," Suze added. "About the party,
and stuff."

Ah, and there was the other thing old friends could
create at will: a tsunami of guilt only half the size of the
one that hit Indonesia. Maybe she was upset about what
happened with that boy. Maybe she wanted to talk about
serious things. I could have spared, like, ten minutes
to listen out of my crappy day of homework and sitting
around being annoyed.

Which is how they wound up at my place that night,
struggling through English, French, and math with copi-
ous amounts of my help. Suze was no longer in a mood to
talk about the party, which she couldn't really remember
much of anyway. My bed was my parents' old king—they

update their furniture about once every five years or so—and we all fit on it, sprawled, with all of our books and everything, contents of our bags spilled out over the duvet.

Maybe blinging up the Ritalin bottle was a bad idea. It just sort of called attention to itself. And maybe carrying it around in my bookbag was an even worse idea—I just thought it would be safer than hiding it somewhere at home. Parents are far more likely to look through your shit when you're not around than they are to conduct a search of your person.

"Oh, cool, what are these?" Suze asked, pouncing on the sparkly bottle like it was the cake in *Alice* that said Eat Me. "Oh hey, I know what this is—the study drug, right? My cousin's taking it for ADHD." And with that she popped off the lid, popped two out, and popped them in her mouth.

"Those could have been cyanide capsules—or anything," Lida pointed out dryly. "My mom keeps all of her different vitamins and pills in the same bottle. You could totally be dead." But she reached over and took two for herself.

"Hey," I said irritably, watching events unfold before I could stop them, "those aren't *free*, you know." I only had, like, ten left.

"First one always is," Suze said with a mischievous grin that would definitely have worked on me if I'd had a penis. And liked girls.

Lida was examining the label now too. "Wow. You'd

need at least four to get a really good high. Unless you
injected them."

"I'm not taking them to get high," I said icily. "I'm taking them because I need them to study."

"Whatever." Lida reached into her back pocket and pulled out a five. "Here. Happy now, Little Miss Banker Woman? They're usually five bucks each but I'm taking the friendship discount."

"Whatever," I muttered back, taking the money. What the hell was five bucks going to get me? One latte? More Ritalin? Full prescription bottles don't exactly fall out of the sky, you know. It's like that sitcom where the kids find a keg on the side of the road, fallen off a truck or something. Manna from heaven. I felt the irritation rising to a crescendo, and had to get out of there. "I'm going to get some Diet Coke—anyone want anything?"

"Water for me, please," Suze said daintily, like she wasn't someone who'd just slugged back two pills with no liquid—someone who was obviously good at it.

I ignored the sounds of Lida grinding hers on a textbook, preparing to snort.

Downstairs Dad and Mom were sitting in the living room, reading magazines with the TV on.

"You getting any actual studying done up there?" Dad asked with an I-know-you're-shitting-me-so-don't-bother-answering look. What a dumb question. I wish there was some way to explain the complexities of everything: how I didn't even want Lida and Suze over, how I was *really* trying to study, how if it were up to me, both of my friends would disappear for a while and come back less needy, how more than anything else I *always* tried to get my homework and studying done. Didn't they ever see that?

"Yep," I answered neutrally, making a beeline for the kitchen.

I heard Mom get up and follow me. Since this was the day of All Shit and Irritation, hackles went up my spine.

Yep. When I turned around from getting glasses out of the dishwasher, there she was, sitting on a stool, leaning over the island, trying to look all friendly-motherly. The glass of wine helped the image: casual, hip, modern mom.

"You guys have all been friends for such a long time," she began.

"Uh-huh," I said, turning my back to her, looking vacantly into the fridge.

"That Lida . . ." She paused and took a sip. "She's not exactly a model student, is she?"

I gritted my teeth and reached in to move stuff around, taking more time so I wouldn't have to face her.

"No, I guess not."

"She's . . . kind of gotten into a bad crowd, hasn't she?"

Bad crowd? Wait, "crowd"? These are the same kids she's known for the last eleven years or longer, not *West Side Story*. Last time I checked, there were no motorcycle gangs in Ashbury.

"Mom . . . ," I said tiredly.

"I'm just saying. I know she's an old friend of yours and all, but people change. Maybe she's not the sort of person you want to surround yourself with right now. Don't you think she's kind of dragging down these 'study sessions'?"

I turned around, trying to keep the anger down. "Yeah? And what about *Susan?*" I demanded.

"Sshhh." Mom frowned and pointed up. "What *about* Susan?"

"Lida's actually got a brain underneath all"—*don't say it*—"all the things going on right now with her." Under the haze of pot. Under the überslacker attitude. Under her shitty clothes and annoying "laid-back" routine. Under the gobs of money she pretends not to have. "Susan really is an idiot."

"Oh, don't say that. Susan will be fine." She pshawed like a grandmother, smiling away with maternal wisdom the things I was too young and dumb to know. My hands began shaking, and my heart did that skippy beat thing—in rage, this time. Somehow Suze managed to charm *everyone*, even my mom, distracting her with the drama and the smiles and the sparklies that trailed after her like a My Little Pony.

I grabbed the Cokes and glasses and headed back upstairs.

"Just think about it, all right?" she called after me. "Your goals right now are school and getting into a good college. Think about things that help that—and people who might distract you."

It took all my effort not to stomp upstairs like an angry teenager. I dropped the drinks off with Lida and Suze, who didn't seem to notice, and headed into the bathroom to clear my head.

Mom was right, of course. Except about Susan. They really were kind of a drag, academically. Like tonight I was going to do my French and math and then spend the rest of the evening reading for the English essay. I always read better when I'm not pressured; Monday nights were great for that, before the crap of the week kicked into high gear.

But what was I supposed to do—just drop them as friends?

What about all that bullshit about high school being the best days of your life, and the friends you make forever?

And what about all those fucking pills they basically stole from me? What was I supposed to do when they were gone? They were my ace in the hole, and I still had one marking period to go. Once again, one Monday night or one exam could decide whether I'd be at a Fortune 500 or assistant managing a B&N.

My heart was beating out of control and all of me was shaking now. So many things affected The Rest of My Life.

I opened the medicine cabinet.

Mom's bottle of Xanax sat there quietly, between the Crabtree & Evelyn aloe vera powder (for Mom) and Nickel Morning-after Rescue Gel (for Dad).

I needed the Ritalin—it was obvious I had undiagnosed ADHD. But I never did anything else, except for a little drinking at parties. This was above and beyond anything I would normally do.

Except this once.

"Thyme!"

I looked up from my place on the floor in front of my locker. There were fifteen whole minutes before classes began for the day and I had them all to myself and *The Grapes of Wrath*. It was the harder of the two books we could choose for our essay in English, but I figured I might be able to spin it into one of those "favorite books" questions on an application—assuming I liked and understood it.

So far, not so much. In fact, it's not for me—the whitest girl in an all WASP all the time school—to say, but something smacked a little, I don't know, anti-Semitic about it. Like merchants and middlemen and shop owners aren't real Americans and basically suck. Or was it anti-Semitic to just assume it's against Jews and not shop owners in general? Some of the philosophy—good people of the earth, etc., etc.—sounded suspiciously like my old friend Communism.

Well, this was what was going through my head, probably the most actually intellectual or academic thing I had thought about in school all year, when Genevieve DeLancie appeared above me, blowing it all to hell.

Genevieve looked exactly like you would imagine a Genevieve to look. Long legs, long hair, long eyelashes. Vaguely Nordic face and beautiful brown eyes boys drown in. She spoke French fluently, won a trip to Paris the summer before in an essay contest, and was a shoo-in for a field hockey scholarship. She dressed somewhere between New York runway and Catholic schoolgirl, making miniskirts and long socks work without looking slutty or girlish.

It appeared that my weekend of irritation wasn't over yet; it was instead rapidly becoming the *week* of irritation.

"So, what was *that* on Saturday?"

"What the fuck are you talking about? What happened on Saturday?" I growled, a little nastier than I meant. Her eyes widened a little in surprise; I'm not the facebiter type, usually. I just hated getting interrupted in my thoughts. In fact, a lot more than I used to. Almost autistically so.

Yeah, I know. Another side effect of the Ritalin. Not very pleasant.

"You and Dave."

I frowned, trying to figure out what she meant. She said it casually, so casually, and kneeled down at the ends of my legs, near my feet, the better to talk. Did it look like Dave and I were flirting? Why was she acting so weird? Did she like him?

Oh, I realized.

"The little deal you guys had going on." She smiled knowingly.

"It wasn't a . . ." I sighed and looked at my watch. Eleven more minutes. "What about it?"

"What was that stuff you gave him?"

"Study aids," I said carefully. Not that I expected her to narc on me or anything, but names have magical powers. You *say* marijuana and Ritalin, and suddenly five minutes of fun at a party take on actionable consequences.

"Oh. Riiiight." She nodded, again knowingly. "So, you don't happen to have any . . . *sleep* aids, do you? Or like, *anxiety* aids?"

I blinked at her.

"I need some Xanax," she admitted, giving in as if I was trying to wait her out. In reality, I just couldn't believe that the head of the French Club was (A), asking for meds, and (B), asking *me* for meds. How did she happen to be watching me and Dave for that one moment? How did she come to the conclusion I had other pills? And more important, how many other people were also watching, coming to their own conclusions?

My heart did that thing which is neither a skip nor a freeze, more like a double-beat palpitation. Speaking of Xanax. This deer-in-headlights could have used some right then.

I opened my mouth, but nothing came out.

"I'm just saying," she said quickly. "If you . . . know where to get some, or whatever. You know. If you need anything, you know, we could trade. I have some codeine left from getting my wisdom teeth out. And my brother has all this ADD stuff he never takes."

"Yeah," I breathed out, trying to sound calm.

"Okay, well, I gotta go, but let me know, okay?" She stood up, trying not to look nervous.

"What do you need Xanax for?" I asked honestly.

I mean, she was so perfect, you just never competed with—or wasted time hating—Genevieve.

"I just need to, you know"—she crumpled for a moment, looking a little sad—"dial down the pressure a little." Then the moment was over; she sort of shrugged her leather hobo bag and clothes back into place and was serene as all get out. "Well, let me know."

"Yeah. Peace out," I muttered under my breath.

But I couldn't stop thinking about the Xanax in my mom's cabinet.

8

The Other Side of Summer

Now you can't afford to fake
all the drugs your parents used to take
—Elvis Costello

The moment Genevieve made me her reliable, safe source of prescription happiness, it was like silent signals hummed and vibrated throughout the fucked-up set of overachievers. Waters were thinly populated in summer, so communication between the pods was slow and broken.

But by the time we all came back to school in September, things really picked up.

Other than slowly building up a clientele—and ensuring a steady supply of R-balls for the fall—summer for me was Kaplan, one course after another, one fake test after another. Even the fake tests take time, just like the real ones. Hours and hours. After the initial anxiety goes away, you're left with mind-numbing boredom.

Kevin theorized that maybe it was like one of those trivia games: If you do it often enough, you cycle back to the same questions. And then it all becomes easy.

Summer was a crappy, almost-full-time job. I worked at my mom's firm; "learning the basics of risk assessment and the hidden costs and theory behind large retail corporations" is what it said on my college applications.

Yep. You guessed it.

It was really just photocopying. And filing.

And answering the phone and redirecting calls when Mom and other people were out. And—I shit you not—*sharpening* pencils. For this asshole Steve. He was always going on about how he wanted to record himself giving lectures and sell them to audiobook companies for seminars.

And that's when he wasn't hitting on me.

What a great introduction to the corporate world.

Summer was coming home exhausted and watching videos with Mom and Dad, which wasn't too bad, because it was friendly and no one talked.

Summer was also parties and trips to the beach. And there was one particularly cool moment, at a party Kevin threw. Uh, the party itself wasn't cool. It should have been, considering his parents were spending the weekend on Block Island and they have a pool. But there was vomiting in the bushes, sex in the guest

rooms, the same kids I had seen every day for the last
fifteen years and would see again every day in the fall,
all acting like total idiots. Suze was supposed to give me
a ride home, but after an hour and a half of searching
every nook and cranny for her and whatever guy was
searching her every nook and cranny, I gave up and
just walked out.

All right, so I was a little buzzed. And maybe a teenage girl dressed for a party shouldn't be walking the
deserted streets in the middle of the night—but I was
Done.

And then Will caught up with me.

"I'll walk with you," he said simply, without chivalry
or obnoxiousness.

I shrugged.

It was a *long* walk. The sort of thing I would have
dreaded if it was during the day and I had no choice. But
it was warm and just before dawn, like a time that didn't
exist, so it didn't matter.

We stopped once to watch the fireflies that filled a
meadow like little alien stars.

"I can do better than that," Will said after we moved on.

"Yeah?"

He took out a can of *hairnet* of all things. Since he
didn't seem to have it at the party, I guess he stole it
from the Moores' bathroom. Kneeling down, he sprayed
something invisible on the black pavement.

Then he lit it.

There are a lot of stupid, dorky things teenagers are supposed to do over the summer, none of which I managed.

But nothing I wished I had done could ever match seeing T-H-Y-M-E blaze up orange in the middle of an empty road on a summer night, putting the fireflies to shame.

Senior year

ᑫ

A New Hope

This is my brother's Ritalin. Ritalin's
    good for studying math or science,
    just don't try to write English papers
    on it or it won't make any sense.
    Enjoy that.
                    —from *Dead Man on Campus*

Fuck them.

Just fuck them *all*.

I slammed my fist into a locker, blinking back the tears.

Fuck. It looked like Genevieve was coming up the hall after me, to talk.

Fuck.

Just an hour ago, senior year looked like it was starting out great:

Economics and statistics (econ).

AP English.

AP French.

PE.

AP Bio.

AP History.

Yearbook: photo editor.

French Club: treasurer.

Senior Booster Club: veep.

Student Council: teacher rep.

National Honor Society: member.

Pretty impressive, no? What college wouldn't salivate over a senior with this curriculum and these extra-currics? I almost didn't make it into AP History—Mom and Dad had to take time out of their schedules to Have a Word with the Teacher. Mr. Volet is a weird, old-fashioned kind of teacher, I guess, who probably should have been at a private school. He told my parents that "I didn't seem to enjoy history" and this class was going to be taught "at college level" and maybe it wasn't the best use of my energy and time my senior year. I think that was the point where my mom lost it and my dad leaned over—way over—into Volet's personal space.

I thought there would be some sort of repercussion; teachers are human too, yeah yeah, we all know that now—but the first day in class Mr. Volet just looked at me and sighed sadly. Which was somehow way worse than putting up with a teacher-grudge all year.

I drew a little sad face next to AP History.

Anyway, as I was saying, this was all great, except

for one thing: I was admiring my schedule and decorat-

ing it during AP English. After the first few minutes of class my attention span dropped to its usual position two points above zero (*What's my median interest level? What's my mean?*). You can OD on Ritalin or Adderall or Strattera (cheaper, 'cause it doesn't get you high) and still not gain enough focus to pay attention in class. Or at least *I* can't.

My fellow students provided little distraction: All of my courses were populated with the complete cast of The Twenty, with an addition or subtraction here and there. I saw the same people for English, Econ, French, even gym.

I had almost no classes with Lida and Suze anymore.

At least Will was in English with me—but he only replied to my notes and whispers with a mild smile, concentrating instead on his drawings and occasional smartass responses to the teacher. Which was a big shame. He had come out the other side of summer smoking hot, like he had suddenly grown into his skin and bones. The baby fat was gone and he let his thick black hair grow out, keeping it shiny and perfect. Even his eyes were sparklier, it seemed like. There was a whole new aura around him.

And no sign that walking home after that party meant anything to him.

Sigh.

"*Thyme.*"

I was distracted out of my first day o' class thoughts by Kevin's nasal twang. He had apparently popped a gasket in the August heat, and now came to school in jackets and ties—unironically, with an attaché and a laptop.

"Yeah?" I said suspiciously.

"I heard you got your parents to get you into Modern Eu."

Yes, he really did say that. Just like a snarky girl in a sitcom.

"Kevin—," I began, unsure of what to say, feeling the familiar warmth of anger that usually stays behind my eyebrows spread to the rest of my body.

"No, no, I think it's great." He put his hand up. "I should have thought of that when I didn't get into phys-h two years ago. It *totally* works."

"I think it's great you've gotten into all these classes," one of his little girl-friends (GPA #7) added. "You've really worked hard."

I honestly couldn't tell if they were being serious and patronizing or insulting and obnoxious. I squirmed with inability to sort out my feelings or express them.

"Stop being a bunch of douches," Genevieve suggested icily. I was surprised and pleased by the unexpected intervention.

"*Thyme* knows what we mean," Kevin added, and that time with a definite dig.

I looked away quickly, afraid I would either cry or leap up and throttle him. Not that anyone else was really

listening; behind me, Meera was reading a book, some-
thing with an alien planet and a half-naked chick on the front, completely oblivious to the teacher and ignored by The Twenty.

Being ignored. What a concept.

Sometimes, that's better than anything, even getting straight A's.

I dragged my palms across my eyes, forcing the tears back in as Genevieve approached. Did everyone think I was an idiot? That I had to work twice as hard as every-one else and trick my way into college?

"Hey, sorry about that, back there," Genevieve said, making a sad sympathy-face.

"Not your fault," I mumbled.

"They sounded like a fucking made-for-TV movie."

We walked together a few moments in silence before she began what I had feared from the moment she defended me.

"So, uh, you still don't have any extra Xanax, do you?"

Yes, The Great Genevieve was going out of her way to defend and talk to Thyme Gilcrest because I was her dealer. *Hurt* and *disappointed* didn't begin to cover the range of emotions I felt; I now had to add *embarrassed* and *angry*.

And it was funny, too, 'cause I had actually been feeling a little guilty about the whole thing—when she had the money, Gen had been buying as much as I felt I could take from Mom's bottle. It was always before social things—parties, swim meets, whatever. With college interviews coming up, she was going to be doped through the season if she wasn't careful.

Too bad I was sick of her shit.

"Gen, you shouldn't be on Xanax," I snapped. "You've got chronic anxiety disorder. You really should be on Paxil, so you can talk to people without being stoned out of your gourd."

Besides reading Suze's—and my parents'—prescription booklets, I was one of those people who watched all of the hospital shows on TV. All that medical stuff was just fascinating, from how doctors talked, to the pills they gave out, to the surgeries they performed. The grosser the better, of course.

Maybe not the best place to learn about drugs, but they seemed to do their research pretty well.

I was prepared for a lot of things: rage, scorn, a flounce and dramatic exit, an end to my relationship with The Most Perfect Girl in School.

Instead, Genevieve blinked at me. "That's not true," she stuttered.

"Yeah, it is—you're always hyperstressed about people. I remember in middle school when you used to throw up before going to dances."

Genevieve blushed and looked around to see if anyone was looking. Sixth grade was a long time before she became cool.

"Kevin needs to take a *Valium* before his oral reports!"

she protested weakly.

This was interesting information, and explained his tendency to zombify out for the rest of the day. I always thought it was just exhaustion.

"Kevin is a douche, as you've said," I dug out two pills and put them into her hand. "This is it. Good fucking luck."

I didn't hate the idea of going to gym next—maybe I could "work it off."

Yeah, maybe if phys ed actually *was* a gym, all tony, with elliptical trainers and pools and hot tubs and a juice bar and cool music playing and pretty people working out in front of mirrors. Sometimes Mom would take me to hers, we'd do a class or two together, and I gotta say it sure as shit beat dodgeball. Clean towels. Clean locker rooms. Individual showers for all.

Saunas.

And if undressing in a locker room full of teenage girls isn't already a cliché about body issues just waiting for denouement, let me fill you in on something that gives this scene a whole new injection of pathos.

Some colleges, it was rumored—and confirmed— actually requested *photos* with applications.

Oh sure, you could opt out. It was totally voluntary.

And I'm *sure* it had no effect on your chances.

People like Suze—who were already flirting with

part-time modeling—had it made. They were used to the camera, beautiful, knew how to make themselves up, and could smile on demand like it was genuine. For the rest of us, it was: body shot or head shot? Candid, showing us working, or frontal, smiling at the camera like a yearbook photo? Should we use the yearbook photo? Make it artsy—or emotional, with the rest of the family? With the rest of the team? With pom-poms? Have the theme match the essay question? Black-and-white? Color? Hologram?

It was the inevitable evolution of college application: SATs are crap, it's your grades. Grades are crap, it's your extra-currics. Extra-currics are crap, it's your looks (or your legacy). Brings a whole new meaning to the term *needs blind*, doesn't it?

So we were all looking around even more than we usually pretended we didn't.

"Hey," Lida announced, holding up a tampon. "Anyone have any Midol or anything? I'm fresh outta brownies."

"Keep your voice down," someone suggested. "A sophomore got suspended last week for going to the nurse with cramps—and having Pamprin on her."

Dorianne (of "rocker chick" fame) nodded. "I heard that too—Michelle Lux-something-or-other. Poor girl. She was bent over in pain and the nurse was like, have you taken anything, and when Michelle showed her the bottle, they sent her home. Zero tolerance."

There were sounds of "No way" and "that's fucking bullshit, man." It was kind of fun. Ten minutes of no social order. Utter lawlessness.

And then Meera killed our buzz.

"Well, she could have just gotten a note from her parents," she pointed out. "How hard would that have been?"

"Aw fuck, Meera," Lida said, rolling her eyes.

"No really," she continued, trying not to sound important, not like a whiny know-it-all. "Besides, there's other ways to manage it. Like, you should start taking Advil twenty-four hours *before* you know you're going to bleed. You want to inhibit prostaglandin production—"

"Ignoring now," Lida said, holding up her hand. Which, while funny, was kind of a bummer. I was actually interested in where Meera was going with that. "Anyone else? Come on, I'm in a lot of pain here. I just started."

Everyone went back to their lockers to dig through their bags and purses. "I have some ibuprofen," the girl to my right offered.

"Tylenol." Someone else held out what I believe was a teeny leather Louis Vuitton pillcase.

"Two of only the finest controlled substances," Dorianne giggled, holding out a packet of the apparently illegal Pamprin.

"Vicodin?" Sonia held out a handful. "I take it for my knee. It'll probably work for cramps."

"Ding! We have a winner!" Lida waited for her prize while the sad little also-rans went back into their Mexx, Prada, L.L. Bean, and Coach bags. This is where it begins, I guess, the myth that mommies have everything in their bags. High school, where suddenly besides your textbooks you have to carry your tampons, cell phones, cramp medications, diet bars, bottles of water, mini makeup kits, contact solution. Mine lacked the diet bar and bottle of water, but made up for it with a pack of gum and some sparkly beads floating around the bottom.

If the world ended right then, we'd probably have enough shit between all of us in the locker room there to last a month.

"You take Vicodin for your *knee*?" I murmured, looking at the fairly inconspicuous single pink bandage that wrapped her injury in question.

"Not all the time," she shrugged. "My dad brought home a bottle from the prison when I first injured it."

Sonia's dad was an administrator in the hospital at Long Hill Penitentiary. She used to be the favorite at sleepovers with gruesome tales of life in the slammer.

And while one might wonder at the thought processes behind a father who brings home a giant bottle of Vicodin for the family medicine cabinet, all *I* could think of was, shit, it's like *everyone* on the planet has access to the drugs that they need except for me.

I had specifically told Suze and Lida to screw off every Monday and Wednesday; they were no-friends, serious-study-nights (Tuesday was Student Council and Thursday was Yearbook, so they were semi-trashed anyway), which I regretted the moment I came home. The house was so fucking quiet I almost prayed for a younger sibling. I wished I could have binged like a normal teen, but having gone through the weight-loss-anxiety thing in middle school, I didn't reward myself with massive amounts of food anymore.

Everyone in The Twenty thought I was a moron. And, apparently, talked about it.

And I really *was* an idiot—that was the hell of it. They were right. I needed to take drugs to study.

And only six Ritalin left.

I picked up the phone, unsure who to call. I could talk to Mom at work, be a little girl for the afternoon and tell her about Kevin's little pity party and my miserable first day at school and cry, but she never had more than a few minutes at a time. I couldn't call Suze or Lida after being so adamant about Monday Suze-and-Lida-Free Day. There was Will, but that would be . . . tricky. He and I still weren't close enough friends that I could just phone him up and shoot the shit, and as for the romantic angle . . . there wasn't exactly one yet. I wasn't ready to ask him out.

I put the phone down and channel-surfed for a while. No good medical shows, not even a documentary about liposuction. I thought about putting in *Moulin Rouge*, my favorite movie and ultimate escape when depressed, but it seemed weird with it still all sunny out. Not really a movie kind of a day. I surfed around online but it was as boring as the TV.

Finally I gave up and just lay on the couch, staring at the ceiling and wishing I could sleep until it was all over or the next interesting thing happened. But napping isn't much of an option when you're on Ritalin.

My cell rang once during the whole time and I scrambled for it, delirious with joy. Then I realized it was just the SAT program I'd ordered, calling me with the word of the day. Ha—it was "enervating." I flipped through a few more vocab words (hackneyed, perfidious, spurious, substantiate, and aesthetic) and answered a couple of practice questions before giving up and rolling over again.

Kevin Moore's phone gave him stock quotes. What a fucking loser.

At eight thirty Mom finally came home, dragging her friend Cassandra along to share a glass of wine before dinner. It was an incredible relief just to have other voices to listen to besides the ones in my head (that sounded suspiciously like Genevieve and the rest of The Twenty). They left their bags on the couch—the *couch*— when they went into the kitchen to gossip. And when Dad came in, he dropped his gym tote on the ground next to the others.

Normally, I wouldn't have even noticed this except

to bitch the next time either one of Them yelled at me for leaving my bookbag in the living room. But I thought about the locker room that morning; the repositories of health, life, and personality that all of our purses had become when we hit sixteen.

And, more important, if ours all contained ibuprofen, Tylenol, and even Vicodin, what did my parental units and Their friends tote around with them?

Dad's gym bag was first, because it seemed the most innocuous. It didn't reek the way you might expect; Mr. Gilcrest was an incredibly tidy man. Sneakers, anti-microbial socks and boxers, dri-weave shorts and top. Quick-dry towel. A ten-dollar bill. Tiny deodorant. Tiny shampoo. Tiny shaving cream, razor, and aftershave. And carefully held in by Velcro straps, tiny vials of the vitamins he was always popping, along with Motrin and Propecia—that's for his not getting bald. One set of straps was surprisingly empty—weird, for Dad. He would have bought something, even a pack of LifeSavers, just to make sure the row was complete. Odd.

I went to Cassandra's Prada next. It was a fucking mess—just like the woman who carried it. D&G sunglasses in an H&M case. Candy wrappers. Slightly beat-up slimline leather checkbook. Credit cards, mints, gum, breath freshener spray (did I mention she was single? Either that or an oral obsessive). Tiny calculator with a cracked solar panel, change purse . . . aha. Jackpot. Prescription bottle.

On the outside, it said PAXIL.

Paxil. My heart skipped a beat, a plan already forming. Maybe I could make up to Genevieve, sell her the stuff I told her she *should* take. . . . I opened the bottle, tapping it into my hand.

And was greeted by a fucking zoo of tiny pills. All different shapes and colors and sizes and milligrams. Some were recognizable, like the happy little Valiums that tumbled easily into my hands, looking like old subway tokens with the hole in the middle. Some actually said Paxil. The rest . . . I had no idea.

But I would soon. Thank you, Internet.

I took a sample of each—and a lot of Paxil. Cassandra would never notice; as demonstrated, she was as organized as my dad was messy (i.e., not at all).

While They ate a dinner of Chinese takeout and Pinot Gris and then Cabernet and then something sweet and digestif-y, I went upstairs, ground up one of my remaining Ritalin, and snorted it.

Why? Why after an entire boring afternoon now suddenly it was night and things were happening and people were home, why now? Why after I said I would never snort anything?

I don't know. I was still miserable. And yeah, some of it had to do with finding the mother lode in Cassie's purse. It opened up a whole new world; like I couldn't believe I'd spent the entire summer in Mom's office and never realized what an easy gold mine the coat closet was. The

weeks would have passed *much* more pleasantly stoned.
And what I didn't want I could trade.

But that's only part of it. I don't know, it was like a switch had been thrown, like, I went suddenly from bored to excited and wanted to keep it, to take it further, I don't know.

I don't know.

I just did it.

10

No Time Like the Present

You grew up before Ritalin-what was that like?

—Jon Stewart

I needed to be proactive. This week I would fix things, change things. Tackle problems head on.

Some of this sudden positive attitude was no doubt a result of the über-Ritalin high I was experiencing. I opened up Excel and began to type. I've always used Excel when I'm starting from scratch, posing questions on a blank page. Real "blank pages," even in Word, are always intimidating. They're so . . . blank. Somehow, with the little gridlines neatly filling up the screen, tasks never seemed too huge or the blankness so empty.

(And some of this anal listing of goals might have been due to the drugs I had been taking as well. I'm no doctor or anything, but it definitely seemed like when

I was on ADHD pills suddenly I got all left-brainy: lists
and flowcharts and careful organizational structure and
study matrices and stuff.)

Problems:
1. Getting into college
   a. School
   b. Extra-currics
   c. Studying for SATs
2. Getting more Ritalin/Adderall/whatever
   a. Making up with Genevieve
   b. Finding a new source
   c. Ensuring supply of new source: having shit
      to trade with
3. Fucking with The Twenty

Okay, that last one was just sort of off-the-cuff, but I
was still smarting from English class and it felt good. Like I
was an evil supergenius coming up with my plans to Take
Over the World and Get Revenge on Those Who Fucked
with Me.

Or was that "Whom"?

I paused, then reluctantly wrote:

4. Will

It's not like there was really a problem there—
there wasn't really even a *there* there. His whole

not-talking-to-me-in-class thing was sort of bothersome. It wasn't like he was paying rapt attention to the teacher. Didn't I rate above science fiction doodles?

Should I just ask him out?

Say it with me: What if he didn't like me back?

Enough. I had to concentrate on the problems I *could* solve.

School and SATs were easy to tackle but boring. I had an idea about what to do with Genevieve, thanks to Cassandra's Paxil. All it would take was an abject apology, some clever wording, and a seemingly heartfelt wish for her to get better, not just feel better.

Okay, so the countdown clock to evil genius was pushed five minutes closer to midnight. Genevieve had pretty much made it clear she was only being my friend because of the pills I sold her. Fine. Sell her pills I would. Xanax you could get almost anywhere. But a steady supply of Paxil? Only from her dear, concerned friend Thyme.

Fucker.

Failing that, I had to have a backup plan, 2 b., "finding a new source."

I started a new spreadsheet and began to list everyone I knew at school, what they were into (or not), what sicknesses mental/physical they had, what they might have access to, and what they were *rumored* to have access to. I don't know what someone in the *Go Ask Alice* era would have done, but get this: In some good public and private schools, up to 30 percent of all high school students are on Ritalin, Adderall, Strattera, Concerta, or some variation thereof. One out of three, so in some ways it was surprising that Lida, Suze, and I were all "officially" ADHD-free.

Finding someone who would trade their shit wouldn't be that hard—it would just take a little questioning, a little keeping my ears open, a little willingness to ask stupid questions . . . and making sure the people were not connected directly to my social circle or The Twenty.

When I finally sat back, I had an interesting table of possibilities. It made me wonder, though: What did people who weren't organized like me do? What did Dave do when one of his sources of weed went to jail or disappeared? I'm sure he didn't go to the Village in the city and talk to one of the "smoke smoke" guys. That way lead directly to juvie hall.

It was kind of ridiculous, really, someone like me, a member of The Twenty, no matter how barely, Student Council rep to the teachers, so carefully organizing my supply of controlled substances.

1. Getting into college (ongoing)

What, like keeping up with my AP courses, acting as the student rep to the PTA, volunteering at the National Honor Society, taking Kaplan prep courses on the weekends, and having my phone send me test questions instead of love letters isn't enough? You want to hear more?

Man, tough crowd.

2. Getting more Ritalin: a. Making up with Genevieve

As soon as the appropriate amount of time had passed—a few days, really—I approached Genevieve in, yeah, the girls' bathroom, as embarrassed and shamefaced as she was when she had first come to me.

"Hey, I just want to apologize for blowing my stack at you the other day," I said, and really meant part of it.

"No problem," she said dubiously, looking into my face for some sort of deception.

"I was way out of line. I should never had said any of those things to you. I just felt terrible about supplying you with that stuff, when that's not what you need. Look, here, peace offering."

I dug out seven Paxil and one zany. *Xanax*, to the uninitiated.

She peered at the little pile of pills, a little less dubiously.

"One week's supply. That should be enough time for you to see if it works. If it does—you know, talk to your parents or something about getting a prescription for it or something. If not, you've got the Xanax for emergencies."

She looked up at me again, in openmouthed,

genuine thankfulness: ice-queen-by-way-of-farmer's-bar
daughter so full of wholesome beauty that it almost
broke my heart. Yeah, I wanted the Ritalin. No question.
But this was win-win: I really was helping her. Wasn't
it terrible that this gorgeous—and basically okay—girl
had a social anxiety problem her parents didn't recognize or do anything about?

"Really?" She took one carefully and held it up to
the light. Whether it was to see if it really said Paxil or
because she had just never seen one before and was
curious, it was hard to say.

"Yeah. Sorry I was such a douche."

I cupped my hand and dumped the rest of them into hers.

"Thanks," she stood there a moment, unsure what to
say. "That's really thoughtful—I thought you were just,
like, being a bitch. I didn't think you were serious about
that whole anxiety thing."

"Yeah, it came out the wrong way."

"Do you—do you want some Ritalin?" she asked.

"Whatever you think is appropriate," I said, shrugging. "We won't even know if the other stuff works."

"I don't have any on me, but I'll get you some, I
promise."

My heart almost stopped. Thanks to my daily habit
and idiot snorting the other night, I only had two left. On
the bright side, midterms were a couple months away
and even without the efficiency the drug provided, I had
all Saturday and Sunday to detox, study for the SATs, and

go to my Kaplan prep course. It just made my situation a trifle more desperate.

My heart was beating so rapidly when I left that I almost wished I had kept the Xanax for myself. Another crappy side effect of the Ritalin. Besides the random sudden heart racing and panic, any little scary thing would set it off.

"You look a little tired tonight," Mom said at the Interviewing Well seminar They took me to. Dad was talking with one of the other dads, legs spread apart and voice deepened, discussing colleges like there was a direct correlation between them and the size of their wangs. "A little worried."

"There's a lot going on," I answered honestly. "A lot on my mind."

"You want an Excedrin or something? To pep you up a little?"

She said it with a concerned, motherly smile, fingers on the clasp of her purse.

3. Fucking with The Twenty

Ireland—1940–1970. Our first oral report was in Modern European History: how deliciously ironic.

"I *hate* these things," I said aloud as Kevin walked by, putting a little shudder into my voice. "I'm always so panicked in front of crowds."

"I am too, sometimes," he responded—patronizingly,
like it was a big revelation, holy shit, THE Kevin Moore
was terrified of speaking in public. Which I guess it
would have been, if I didn't have prior knowledge.

"Really? I can't believe it." *Do not gag, Thyme: Go
along with it.* He nodded sagely. "You should do what I
do," I suggested brightly. "Take a Valium. It really makes
the whole thing easier."

"Uh, yeah," he said, suddenly flushed and looking
nervous. He was the worst cross of guilty pill popper and
snob: high-strung enough to take drugs, too holier-than-
thou to admit it.

If only there was someone he could trust, someone
who understood, who could safely supply him.

"I'll give you a couple, if you want," I offered.

"Oh, ah, maybe. Maybe I'll take you up on that," he
said slowly, as if he were thinking about it.

"Maybe." Ha.

It was like a freshman saying "maybe" to a bottle of
fucking import at her first real party. There was no way
he was going to be able to say no when the time came.

Why would I offer these precious precious pills to one
of the biggest boobs in The Twenty, free?

Hey, as Lida said—the first ones are *always* free.

And speaking of Lida and Suze, although I didn't put
them down on paper, they were in bold letters on my
mental list. I felt bad about blowing them off all the time

and I missed the three of us hanging out. Sure, they could be annoying in their own ways, but—you know.

Nor did they disappoint me: When I called and e-mailed and apologized, Lida suggested we all go to the movies. Suze even let me bitch about my awful first day of school without interrupting too much to talk about herself. There was a crappy comedy playing that looked like it would do the trick—*House Rulez II*. So cheap they couldn't afford Ashton Kutcher.

A ginormous portion of the crowd was from Ashbury High—it was like a fucking organized event. Popcorn got thrown, people shouted out things at the screen. It was like we were already in college or something.

Suze got up in the middle of the movie to pee—she always did that, after drinking gallons of 7UP—and didn't come back for a long time. It sort of bothered me in the back of my head, but I didn't think about it until later. I was too busy fighting Lida for the giant purple SweeTARTS and wondering why Will wasn't there.

Wednesday was English again, first class, and though my spirits were bolstered up a little, it was still like returning to the scene of a crime. Where I was the perp instead of the victim. I know I should have walked in proudly, defiantly even, but me against a gaggle of Twenty ringleaders is not a winning proposition. I kept my head down and tried to avoid everybody's eyes but Will's (and his were engaged in his latest sketch, weird tentacled things coming up out of the ocean in what

looked like a quaint New England village).

Unfortunately, Dorianne of the Twilight Zone decided this was the perfect time to talk to me.

"I'm soooooo depressed," she said dramatically, loudly. Hitting the back of my chair.

Yeah, well, no shit. She wanted to be in a goth band. Being depressed was, like, her job.

"Yeah?" is what I actually said. I kept it as neutral as possible; of all the people I "shouldn't surround myself with" as a senior applying to colleges, Dorianne Teddy was a prime walking, talking disaster of an example.

"I can't get up in the morning, and when I get home in the afternoon, I just sit around. Don't feel like doing anything."

"Yeah, well, that's because you're a fucking narcissist bipolar depressant." As I said, I'm not normally a face-biter. It was the Ritalin talking.

"*What* did you just call me?" she demanded, leaning forward.

The bell hadn't rung yet, and didn't seem like it ever would. Tildenhurst was still on the school phone, turned toward the wall and holding one hand slightly over her face as if we could lip-read her whispery, spidery words. Rumors already surrounded her—that she was a lesbian, that she was a witch, that her daughter in college was a schizo. Sonia said she came to the counter at CVS once with a bottle of black nail polish and a tube of K-Y, which really could have confirmed any of the three.

"A narcissist bipolar depressant," I repeated, sighing.

"What does that mean?" she asked, a little less angrily.

"Well, uh"—I cleared my throat—"you don't really have trouble talking to other people. . . ."

"No."

"So you probably don't have social anxiety disorder."

"Yeah? No."

"Sleep issues do sound like serious depression. . . ."

"Yeah?" She pushed her chair closer, so close I could see the little ridge on her nose where her parents had it, uh, tucked.

"Yeah, I would probably say bipolar."

"You got the fix?" she asked, putting her hand out.

"What?"

"I know you and Genevieve have this arrangement going on, Rock-and-Roll Doctor. What do I need?"

A good solid kick in the ass, is what my granddad would have said.

"Why don't you go see a shrink?" Every other kid—and I think everyone in The Twenty except me—went to one, or a therapist. But not a social worker. That was for low-class folk with Disturbed Children.

Why wasn't I seeing someone? My idiot parents thought I was sane.

And sometimes, looking at the people around me, I almost believed them.

Dorianne blushed. "My parents . . . don't really

believe in that sort of thing. They think it's for *really* crazy people."

I knew exactly what she meant.

Overheard in the cafeteria:

"Nahh, I don't have any Ritalin or anything any-more."

"Didn't you used to?"

"Oh, yeah. I was misdiagnosed as having ADD for ten years. Then they made me take this test again, before I started studying for the PSATs and shit. Turns out I was just lazy."

4. Will

"You didn't go to the movie with everyone the other night. I totally thought you'd be there."

It was a little hard to be casual when I had been mulling over my "perfect opening line" for several days. But I had just taken my second-to-last pill a few minutes before, and the initial effects were pretty immediate. Call it psychosomatic if you will, but I'd be taking sugar pills if someone convinced me that it would increase my study focus.

"Yeah?" He stopped his bored-drumming routine and turned in his seat to look at me, raising one eyebrow. Crap. He was so accidentally sexy. I wish I had that sort of confidence. His hair, pulled in its usual loose ponytail over one shoulder, gleamed with a comic book shine like he had drawn it in. Every girl I knew would kill for that hair. "Why would you think that?"

"I don't know. It was funny. You're funny."

"I am?"

"Sometimes." This was either reaalllly slow flirting, or not going anywhere. Time to plunge in, like the artless girl I was. "Hey, why don't you ever talk to me anymore?"

"What are you talking about?" he asked with a snort, the old Will, the sarcastic, perpetually pissed-off Will I knew.

"I don't know. This summer—" I didn't know what to say. The walk home after the party together had been so magical. Maybe part of it was because it was an unanswered question, a suggestion left hanging—but part of it just *was*. And I didn't know how to put that into words in the cold fluorescent light of day in school. And I didn't know if he'd felt the same way at the same time, or if he was just drunk. "I don't know," I said again. "I thought we really, uh, I don't know, connected at Kevin's party."

"Yeah," he said, shrugging. I was surprised, but there wasn't an opening, anywhere to go from there.

"So . . . ?" I prodded.

He looked at me unblinking, then turned his attention to the previously abandoned pencil slash drumstick and began rolling it around on the desk. It didn't come

across as little-kid-embarrassment-staring-at-the-ground,
though. It felt like there was something unpleasant he
didn't want to tell me.

"I don't know," he finally said, slowly. "I'm not ignoring you. You've . . . got your posse, and the grinds you
roll with." He rolled his eyes at Kevin and Genevieve
and other little Twenty-ites; all were laughing at something, bright-eyed and beautiful for a moment—definite
Ivy material.

So *he* thought of me as a real, full member of The
Twenty? Someone more accustomed to booster club sessions with Genevieve and dating people like our hockey
star—high, wide, and handsome-with-a-4.0?

Did everyone else in the senior class think that too?

That I really was one of the beautiful people destined
to do fabulous things at great colleges with fantastic
yearbook quotes?

A little chill went over me, something that might
have been very much like self-esteem. Because the
corollary to that revelation was obvious now: *Everyone*
in The Twenty probably thought they were desper-
ately jockeying for position and barely hanging on. It
was nasty, monkey survival—and Kevin might feel as
crappy as me sometimes.

Right?

When my brain had finished its little Special Moment
of Self-Discovery, I refocused on Will, but he already had

his notebook open and was hunched over, shading what looked like a laser turret on a UFO.

Moment over.

"And . . . we need to fill up time slots at the Connecticut Loves Reading day at West Farms next Sunday. Who wants the two-to-three-o'clock slot, for preschoolers?"

"Oooh oooh, pick me," I said, waving my hand like a preschooler. Only a few people in the room smiled—the National Honor Society was a tough crowd.

It was dark out; this meeting was called in between Model U.N. and the PTA weekly, after all the usual sports and shorter-term extra-currics. I had been at school for ten hours and wouldn't be going home for another two. My life was being defined by the fluorescent lights, which looked even worse against the night sky.

"Okay, settle down," the librarian/NHS coordinator said with what might have been the prehistoric beginnings of a smile, writing my name down. "Just submit the name of the book you want to read from by next Tuesday. All right, on to the holiday dance. . . ."

"HEY."

I jumped, Suze's head suddenly right next to mine. Its placement there was wrong for a whole number of reasons, starting with the fact that Suze wasn't a member of the National Honor Society and ending with the fact that her hair was tickling my nose.

"What?" I hissed back, trying to pay attention to which committees were being formed.

"I need to talk to you."

There was a little bit of booze on her breath, but her eyes were big with worry. It must have been serious; she would have had to come *back* to school to find me, something Susan Merritt never would have done under normal circumstances.

Cursing her a little in my head but caving in to the inevitable, I did that weird half-bow sneak-out thing people do in the movies which doesn't really help at all. It looked like I was going to graduate from school without ever having been on a Dance Decorations Committee. I wasn't normally into kitsch, but was it so much to ask?

We journeyed to the closest girls' room—not the one where I pushed Paxil on Genevieve. It took Suze a while to warm up to the subject; she immediately began to fix her hair and make funny monkey lips to examine her teeth better. I pulled out my Ramy lip gloss and applied it daintily, rubbing my lips together afterward. I had fallen so far behind on fashion and makeup trends—maybe I should have stopped dressing so conservatively. Prairie (slutty) chic was supposed to be coming back. As soon as I had time to think again . . .

"That color looks so good on you," Suze said, taking a breath and grabbing the (small) bellyfats out of her pants to look at them.

"Thanks," I said, about to move on to the obvious question.

"So I think I'm pregnant."

I'd like to say that this came as a complete surprise.

"Suze . . . ," I said slowly.

"Last week. At the movies? When I left?" She bit her lip and did her big scared brown eyes thing, which was also a total drama queen thing, but I guess she had the right to be dramatic about this.

"You took the pregnancy test then?"

"No, I had a quickie with Tommy Halder in the bathroom."

You know how teenagers are always, like, Oh My GOD this is the worst thing EVER and my life is OVER and I can't BELIEVE my FRIEND did this I thought she was SMARTER oh my GOD, etc., and go into a dramatic spin, filling up pages of their blog, crying their eyes out and telling everyone they're not supposed to?

I only *wish* I could have felt those things.

Instead, I was torn between laughing violently, vomiting, and just sighing.

"You had sex with Tommy Halder in the women's bathroom at the Cineplex," I said slowly, hoping she would correct me, hoping I'd heard wrong.

She shook her head. "Nope. The *unisex* one, the handicapped one, you know."

"Well, it *is* larger," I agreed, not sure what else to say.

"See? That's what I was thinking," she said, throwing her arms around wildly, playing it up for laughs.

"Susan H. Merrit, you are a total fucking idiot," I said, really meaning it.

"I know," she said, nodding. Then she began to cry.

She didn't cry pretty, that was one thing about Suze. Her sparkly eyes and high brow got all red and blue, and bags appeared instantly, thick and heavy as stormclouds.

"What . . ." I didn't know where to begin. "What was such a turn-on about *House Rulez II* or Tommy that you suddenly had to fuck him—in the bathroom—without a condom? And I thought you were on the pill!"

"I don't know, I was a little bored, and we both were going to the bathroom at the same time, and it was like we had the whole lobby to ourselves, and I always thought he was kind of sexy, and . . ." She dissolved into a puddle of tears.

"And the pill . . . ?" I repeated.

"I think I missed a few. I don't know, I just sort of forgot."

The girl who rations out her cigarettes so carefully couldn't be bothered to take her pill on a regular basis, which even comes in a convenient, colorful compact with numbered days.

But she was crying, and I put my arms around her. She clung to me like a child, sobbing and ugly.

Tracy Lynn

Name	Circle	Needs?	Can Provide	Notes
Kevin	The Twenty	Stick removed from his ass/Valium	Amusing distraction/revenge	
Genevieve	The Twenty	Xanax, Paxil	Ritalin	
David	Stoner	Weed	Weed and . . . ?	
Lida	See above	See above	See above	Probably avoid. Don't mix friends and business.
Suze	Undefined	Celexa Wellbutrin	Celexa Wellbutrin	Ditto above, except maybe get some stuff from her for Dorianne
Dorianne	Goth/Freak	Serotonin Reuptake Inhibitors	???	
Jun	Partyer	???	???	Out of my league
Hal Pelling	Jock/Stealth The Twenty?!?!	???	Adderall	Diagnosed w/ADHD for five years
Karenna Roberts	Über-rich	Nothing	Strattera	Note: Web says it's not an "analeptic" like A, R, and Concerta ???
Frederick Groven	Drama Geek /JUNIOR	A fucking life	Ritalin	

11

Withdrawal

It was the greatest feeling I ever had,
followed very abruptly by the worst
feeling I ever had.
                                    —from *Blow*

Hey, remember how depressed I was that day when I thought Genevieve was only my friend because I gave her Xanax? And how upset I was that everyone in The Twenty probably thought I was an idiot and didn't belong there? And how awful it was that my best friend was pregnant? And stupid?

That was all nothing, nuh-uh-uh-uh-thing, compared to my accidental experiment in going cold turkey off of Ritalin.

And remember how I figured, okay, so I only had enough for the week, I'd be all right, the weekend would be a good time to detox anyway? I could stay home, drink a lot of water (or water and honey and lemon and hot sauce or whatever it is my mom and Cassandra did to flush their fat), soak in the tub, put cucumbers on my eyes, and do all the sorts of spa-y substance abuse recovery stuff you read about.

Hys-fucking-terical.

It started innocently enough; I woke up feeling a little tired, like I hadn't gotten enough sleep—even though it was a full nine hours. I forced myself to get up anyway and went downstairs for the goddamn pancakes, feeling a thousand years old, my joints actually creaking a little. There were undefined pains in my back and legs, like I had slept funny. I didn't fall into the Saturday Morning Role the way I was supposed to; instead, I grunted like a crazy homeless person when Dad shoved the pan o' cake in my face. I fell gracelessly into my seat and squinted at everyone.

"Hangover, honey?" Mom asked with a nervous laugh. They knew where I was last night. Upstairs, doing homework. I had taken my last Ritalin two nights before and the going was beginning to get tough.

I grumbled unintelligibly and poured some orange juice, but suddenly didn't feel hungry. Not sick to my stomach, just—not hungry. Like it was less than interesting. Which wouldn't really have been a problem if I didn't have to force myself through a whole pancake and gobs of sticky cold syrup just to keep Dad happy and feeling like he was a fun, contributing member of the team.

"Why don't we all do something today?" Mom

suggested, suddenly June Cleaver and Martha Fucking Stewart all in one. Unfortunately, ideas failed to materialize.

Dad made a grunting noise not dissimilar from mine. "I'm meeting Dan at the club later for tennis. You could come. I'll tell him to bring his partner."

"What about Thyme?"

"She can bring a friend. Or you can call Cassandra."

Like *playing tennis* at the club was a rare treat. I'll tell you what was a treat—*eating* there, with enough forks at each place setting that you could start your own restaurant. Crystal glasses and linen napkins. Soaking in the hot tub. Checking out the hot crews during sailing season. Gawking at diamonds on the Really Rich.

Not playing tennis.

"Gotta study," I said around the last mouthful of pancake, which took a Zen master's effort to swallow. I brought my coffee with me upstairs, the monster returning to its den with its prize.

"Well," Dad said, like one of those BBC characters.

Upstairs I lay on my bed and . . . there's no real way to describe it. Like I was in a medieval torture chamber or something. A several-ton block of granite was being slowly lowered onto me. Really—it felt like an actual, physical weight was pressing my body into the earth. I laid myself out as flat as I could on my bed, trying to sink into it, spread out the pressure. Finally I rolled off onto the ground, letting the cool wood of the floor support me.

Getting up was completely out of the question. I couldn't move. Everything was so fucking hard. Just turning my head was exhausting.

When the phone rang it hurt, like the vibrations were invading my head.

My heart felt cold. I know that sounds stupid. I was frozen but couldn't shiver.

I said to myself: This is ridiculous, Thyme Gilcrest. Get up and do your goddamn SAT prep questions before the Kaplan study session.

Spidery knockings on the door:

"Is everything all right?" Mom called.

"Yeah," I managed to blurt out.

And that was enough. She was gone.

And then I began to cry.

Even that was too hard—one tear came out and I began sobbing like Suze had, but there were no more actual tears after that first one.

I've had depressed days before, but it was never, ever like this.

The time to go to Kaplan came and went and I was still on the floor.

Minutes passed slowly, and every moment was agony. There were voices in my head. Loud. Not like I really heard them outside myself, or thought they were from Satan or anything; they were just my own thoughts,

racing around and around and saying shit about me.
Like this:

you should get up you lazy fuck this is why you're
not really a member of the twenty this is why
you're not going to a good school useless little girl
can't do anything without a drug your dads right
about you being a dummy not that it matters your
friends are going to rat you out everyone knows
you sell the drugs you need you suck you suck
you suck

It was like I was stuck in *1984*. They had figured out the best way to torture me: with my own thoughts. Over and over again. I couldn't get away.

And I believed every word.

I finally got up only because of the incredible stomach cramps that had steadily grown as the afternoon went on. I managed to haul myself to the bathroom and hung over the toilet, praying for the relief and release of endorphins that was sure to follow.

But nothing came, I didn't even really heave. I just cried more, leaning against the basin like I was sick drunk.

Eventually I gave up, went back to my room, and tried to do some of the online SAT practice sessions so the afternoon wouldn't be a total waste. Not only didn't I have the interest or heart for that, I didn't even feel like surfing. Just switching pages on the screen made me more nauseated.

Looking at the people who were on instant messaging, I realized I would rather have stuck a knife through my eyes than talk to anyone. Regardless of how lonely I felt.

Seeing Suze's name started me crying again, thinking about how stupid she was, and how pitiful, really, and how avoidable it all was. And for just a moment of real heavy crying, I thought about telling Mom. Everything. I mean, isn't that what parents are for? To take the worry off you? To let you know what's important (worrying about good grades) and what's not (worrying if that hot guy from Lewis Prep will come down out of the holy ether to ask Sonia to the formal, not you). To calm you. They're like the biblical scapegoat, right? You tell them all the horrible things and cry in their laps and they take it all away from you.

And maybe you get in trouble later, and maybe they punish you for taking study drugs and your friend hates you for her dad finding out she's pregnant, but that's later, and this terrible pain you feel meanwhile is over.

Yeah, I wised up after a while.

My life would be officially O.V.E.R. if they knew I was doing Ritalin. And Suze's dad would have her committed to a nunnery or thrown out of the house. Think I'm exaggerating? He had some pretty strong illusions about his Princess, and some equally strong ideas on how teenagers should be punished these days.

Besides, I hadn't really laid my head on Mom's less than ample breasts or sat in Dad's lap for several years.

It would just be . . . kind of awkward now.

So I lay there and felt sick, like I was dying or had the flu or something, but the symptoms weren't real. Does that make sense? It's like my body hurt without hurting, like I had a fever without being hot. Like I was trapped in my own skin.

I wanted to just cut it all out. With a knife. I would have done almost anything to end the pain and the thoughts and the misery.

I've never really had suicidal thoughts before, or at least no more than any average undepressed teenager. Not like this. The thought of not having to bear it, of not having to think about Suze or college or SATs or Will or The Twenty, was almost overwhelming in its beauty.

If I had a gun or a knife in my hand, I might have actually used it.

At some point I heard the door slamming and Them yelling, "See you—we'll be back later—you can invite someone over for dinner, order a pizza if you want," which meant They wouldn't be coming home until late in the night.

And then the house was silent, and it was just me.

Sometime after midnight I finally came downstairs and sat on a stool at the island in the kitchen, slowly but thoroughly finishing off a carton of milk—no glass required. It felt like I had been through a long, drawn-out battle or extremely sick. I was weak and exhausted, but no longer felt like killing myself. Just enough back to good old Thyme to realize how I had wasted the day.

All because I ran out of pills.

Which I was never, ever going to do again.

12

8 Mile Road

You can sift me, cut me, I'll turn you
   to a junkie
I'm the number one seller in the whole
   fuckin' country
                    —50 Cent/Tony Yayo

If only that was the end of it. If only one lost day, one horrible twenty-four-hour period of depression and misery was the sum total of what the universe figured I owed.

First off, the depression, though slightly less awful and extreme, lasted through the next day.

And second . . . well, let's just say that nothing makes you feel more like a junkie than dealing with a dealer.

The person on the list of ADHD-positives who best fit the category of knowing-well-enough-to-talk-to but not enough to be friendly with (and therefore unlikely to be in my gossip circles) was junior drama geek Freddy Groven. I figured the best place to find him was near his lair, and after school was rewarded by finding him sitting on the floor of the auditorium, reading a script all furrowed-brow serious, waiting for someone to notice him.

"Hey," I said. "I hear you have Ritalin."

That's it. That's really it. Are you listening, parents and teachers? No meeting in a deserted parking lot, no codewords like "tree" or "4:20," no need to go to the Bad Kids or the Wrong Side of the Tracks.

"Sure." He looked at me carefully before reaching into his bag, like he was scanning me: The doofus actor vanished, suddenly transformed into an X-ray machine or one of those nasty sales associates at an expensive store who can tell immediately which girls are there with Mommy's Credit Card and which are likely to leave a lot of deodorant marks on clothes they can't afford.

By the time he reached into his bag, that look was suddenly gone, replaced with a goofy would-be cool smile.

"How many do you need?"

Not want, please notice. *Need.*

Suddenly I was getting irritable. I was standing over him in this big deserted room, and somehow found myself at the other end of the telescope, small and upside down.

"Uh, four or five, I guess."

"I can give you four."

Another thing I didn't understand at first—didn't he

have an unlimited supply? I thought I heard a full bottle in there.

Then I got it: *I can give you four. I could* give you five. But I am giving you four. For now. It was a little power thing. Just letting me know how much I needed him, and how in control he was.

"How much?" I pulled my change purse out of my bag and began counting through the singles like I was getting a soft drink or a box of tampons.

He frowned, calculating.

"Forty," he decided.

"WHAT?"

He shrugged.

I almost stamped my foot, I almost dropped the purse.

"That's ten dollars a pill," I protested. "Everyone else sells them for five or *less.*"

He shrugged. "So get it from everyone else. I'm saving up for the new PlayStation. And you look like you really need it."

Another time, another circumstance, I might have been offended—was he referring to the circles under my eyes or limpness of my hair or the general un-put-togetherness of the usually Happy Monday Morning Me?

My stomach burned and filled itself with acid. This junior, this pipsqueak *nothing* class clown, had looked me over, figured me out, summed me up, and finally overcharged, knowing that I would pay.

He also knew exactly where he ranked in my

world—and made it apparent that I was going to pay for that discrepancy.

"I'll take three," I said, trying to keep the shakiness out of my voice while putting a hefty dose of chill in. That was almost all of my week's allowance.

Freddy very obviously removed the one pill and put it away, taking an extra-long time while I stood there, money in my hand, alone in the dark.

He made me lean down, not making any effort to hand them up to me. "A pleasure doing business," he said with a big grin.

I took the long walk of shame silently up the aisle of the auditorium, without even any little clicking shoe noises that might have comforted me, thanks to the otherwise stylin' black-and-pink Nikes that hushed my footsteps like I was in church. I wanted to throw the double doors wide open in anger, letting them bang against the wall. Instead I cracked the left one just enough to let me through, to keep the rectangle of light as small as possible, to keep it from touching Freddy.

On the other side I opened my hand—sweaty and tightfisted, I had almost pulverized the pills I had just paid so dearly for, like whatever the opposite of Superman turning coal into diamonds is. I felt like puking.

Never, ever would I let myself feel like this again.

Never would I be in some idiot little underclassman's, some retarded no one's power again.

Never.

Overheard at the Gilcrest household:

"Idiot," Dad snapped at the white, unrepentant guy on the screen.

"Did he sully the name of your great team?" Mom asked, rather drolly. Besides His University, Dad has His Team for each of His Sports, His Political Party, and His Car Company.

"He got *caught*."

"So it's okay to shoot up testosterone for your team as long as you don't get caught?"

"I think it's a *terrible* example to young kids. But everyone's batting so high because of all the freaky cocktails they're on. Should this asshole suffer just because he's normal?"

For some reason, that remark stung this little eavesdropper. I'll let you figure out why.

"Maybe there could be two leagues," Mom suggested with a twinkle in her voice. "One for good old-fashioned baseball—no drugs and no designated hitter—and one with genetically mutated, steroid-enhanced superpeople. *Extreme* baseball."

"Fucking American League," Dad said, taking a hefty swig of beer and swallowing a vitamin.

"Hey." I caught up to Dorianne in front of her locker, where she was carefully strapping a guitar to her back with an un-goth shiny silver strap that looked suspiciously like a belt, one from Urban Outfitters. Kudos to the recycled-clothing effort.

I had a plan: I could use my powers for *good* this time, have less to feel guilty about, *and* turn a nice cash profit all at once. It was win-win-win.

"Are you serious about treating your depression?"

"You sound like a fucking drug ad on TV." She looked over some papers that were clipped to her locker door; they looked like sheet music but without normal notes. "Why do you suddenly care?"

"Look, you want help or not?" I said, unconsciously shrugging a little like Freddy.

She rolled her eyes, silver sparkles falling from her lids like bits of glass. If I had her lashes, I wouldn't bother with any shadow at all.

"Do you even *know* what it's like to be depressed?"

In a little place we like to call Thyme's Universe, Our Hero lost a weekend because of one of the worst lows she's ever had, had to buy drugs at exorbitant prices from a nasty wannabe pimp-ass junior, and will soon be taking her best friend to get an abortion.

"Yes. Yes I do," I said, thinking about Saturday.

Something must have come through in my voice.

"All right," she said, finally looking at me. "What's the deal?"

"Do you have stomach problems?" I asked, thinking of Zoloft. Dad was on it briefly. It turned him into a reasonably happy father figure for a week or two, but then

we all had to watch as he vomited up a barely digested
steak at the dining table.

"Uh, I get cramps easy, if that's what you mean," she
said with far less embarrassment than I would have.

Besides her now steady diet of Celexa and Wellbutrin,
Suze had been on Prozac, Zoloft, and Lexapro—which is
a version of Celexa but a lot more expensive, with a lot
fewer side effects. She said Zoloft made her unable to do
math—it certainly seemed to destroy her memory. And
Prozac was just so . . . old school.

"I guess I would say Celexa, then."

"What's that?"

"It's like a"—I dove for the SAT word—"*panacea*
antidepressant. Everybody takes it for stress and mild
depression. And it won't upset your stomach." I really
did sound like a fucking TV ad, but as soon as I said it,
it felt right.

Dorianne cocked her head, thinking about it.

"Will it affect my creativity?"

I chose my words carefully. "Do you write more songs
when you're, you know, upright and able to write songs,
or when you're lying in bed staring at your Coldplay
posters?"

Okay, maybe not that carefully.

But apparently it was the right thing. "You really *do*
know a lot," Dorianne said appreciatively, "about medicine and shit. Can you get me some?"

"I'll see what I can do," I promised.

"And hey, if that doesn't work out, some uppers would do nicely," she added brightly. She may have been joking, but it was doubtful.

The rest of the week wasn't quite so dramatic, or depressing, or humiliating—or productive. I delicately tried to talk to Suze about her, uh, issue, but she avoided it and then me and Lida like the plague whenever we brought it up. According to my calendar, this was going to become a problem soon. We would have to think of some way of confronting or intervening pretty quickly.

I broke the pills I had in half to make them last longer—no more snorting—and to cut down my dependence. If I was going to come down again, it wouldn't be as bad as Black Saturday.

Overheard at Lida's party (to celebrate her dad's new entertainment system):

"Holy shit, Thyme. I didn't know you toked."

"Jesus, it was one hit. I'm just being social."

"*Thyme is a stoner, Thyme is a stoner. . . .*"

"Okay, here, loser. I don't even *want* this other one— Dave gave it to me a while ago and it's still got that 'new joint' smell."

"*Dave* rolled it? Yeah, sure I'll take it. What do you want?"

"What do you have?"

"A bunch of Ritalin—I never take it. How's that?"

A week after Black Saturday I was—yeah, laugh at the irony—reading to kids at the mall.

You know, it was actually kind of fun?

They sat the reader on this little stage directly under the skylight, near the fountain, and put down shaggy rugs for the kids to lie out on. They even gave us body mikes. There's something really special about having the undivided attention of forty kids who would normally be running around, playing their Game Boys, flipping channels, or pulling one another's hair out.

I read *Next to an Ant* by Mara Rockliff, and made little ant motions with my fingers that the kids really liked. Too bad there's no money in professionally reading books to children; it would be a lot more fulfilling than risk assessment.

Afterward, parents and teachers and complete strangers came up to me to thank me and congratulate me and tell me what a wonderful service I was doing for the community. I blushed. I glowed. Even if the rest of my fifteen minutes of fame were like this, small and community oriented and personal, I'd be happy.

There was only one sour note. On my way to the bathroom I noticed a pack of boys huddled in the corner, standing together, facing inward like a protective ring of triceratops. There was an aura of *disobedience* surrounding them, of looking over their shoulders and nasty giggling.

I drew closer, intrigued. Would it be a porn mag or the result of some theft?

Five little blond and thug-hat-covered heads looked up half in defense, half in guilt, a bottle of NyQuil in two hands at once, frozen while being passed.

"You have *got* to be kidding me," I said, unable to stop myself. Everyone knew about freshmen overdosing on cough medicine because it's supposed to get you high—but middle schoolers? Little boys?

Without thinking, I swiped the bottle away from them. "This is really stupid, and bad for you," I said, somewhat lamely.

What right did someone who trades in prescription drugs have to intervene like that? I couldn't say. It was all instinct and reaction. All I knew was that ten-year-olds were gulping back toxic amounts of something that was, well, potentially quite toxic. Call it maternal urges, if you will.

"BITCH!" one of the little boys shrieked at me.

Charming, no? The amount of bile and hatred from such a sweet little Connecticut angel was overwhelming. Where did it come from? Where did he get the ability to talk to an older person, a complete stranger, like that?

And what was so awful in their short, middle-class lives that they had to get high? At the *mall*? With *cough syrup*?

We went to church the next day ('cause Grandma was in town)—but it was cool. I hadn't been in a while, and

no, it didn't just have to do with getting to dress up a little
differently (pastels and pearls, like a diminutive Easter).
Sometimes it sort of nags in the back of your head, like
not exercising in a while. And then you hear the sermon
and you're like, shit, no wait, I forgot how much I hated
this. You can run your eyes only so many times over the
same stained-glass windows you've been looking at for
almost twenty years (though stoned, they'd be just brilliant).

The guys were cute, I have to say, very hot and
prep school in their Sunday best jackets and ties.
(Tommy Halder was ironically absent. Probably out
getting another girl pregnant. A pox on him.) The pews
were filled with perfect examples of white Anglo-Saxon
Protestants in their natural habitat. Some could have
been models. Some could have used smaller chins and
larger brains.

And none of them interested me like Will did.

My usual church musings were interrupted when I
caught Suze, three rows up, bent over and crying, hiding
it in her prayer book.

13

Lady Xanax

So many friends but nobody calls
Can't be alone when the darkness falls
—Duran Duran

In middle school there were almost no classes the week before the Spring Formal. Everyone was on some committee and the whole school was dedicated to producing the night, from home economics overseeing the catering to math classes working out ticket price and cost of flowers. It was a grand frenzy that all led up to the day of, when everyone left school early to get their hair done.

In high school, SAT week was kind of like that.

Some people actually stayed out for a few days, taking intense one-on-one tutoring sessions or crash courses, trying to get that last ten or twenty points. Teachers devoted every class to vocab refreshers and quizes, SAT-appropriate math problems, reading and comprehension skills. There were assemblies about game-day performance (get a good night's sleep beforehand, drink plenty of fluids, no partying), and open sessions with the school counselor for students who felt Stressed.

Which was everyone, by the way. But no one had time to go.

Some parents had already signed their kids up for "makeup" test days (do-overs) two and three weeks in advance, just in case, assuming the worst.

I don't think I did any homework that week—even Mr. Volet gave up trying to teach for teaching's sake, playing DVDs of something called *Blackadder* instead and having us pick out what was historically right and wrong in each episode.

Friday night there were lots of study groups, but I went straight home and spent a quiet evening watching TV, taking a bubble bath, and Trying Not to Think About It. I probably should have stayed completely out of Their way and spent the entire night upstairs, but I sort of had the urge for low-key company. You know. Like family.

"Shouldn't you be studying?" Parental Unit 1, Male, demanded the moment he came in from his rec room (it started out as a study and then became an office, but the current fad was playrooms for grown-ups. I would have been actually interested if there were a foosball table for the retro effect, but he had only a TV and a workbench and a mini-fridge and other stuff like that). He had a beer in one hand, his bottle of vitamins in the other, and was in total frat jock mode: wearing a carefully frayed, oversize His University T-shirt and khaki shorts, sockless docksiders on his feet.

My blood began to boil, but hey—at least it was anger, not fear.

"I studied all summer and the past two months straight for this," I explained calmly. "Tonight the best thing I can do is chill out and get a good night's sleep."

"Well, if that's what you think is best for you," he said doubtfully, taking a long pull from the bottle.

He looked like he might have had more to say on the matter, but I turned up the volume on the TV.

Mom saved the moment by coming in with a tray of decaffeinated Mexican coffee (whipped cream, vodka, Kahlúa) and giving me one, having sensed the nervous tension and putting her motherly urges aside (you know, urges like not encouraging her teenage daughter to drink). She even put sprinkles on it.

"I used the full-fat whipped cream," she confided, clinking my mug with hers, a little toast. I grinned, incredibly grateful for the interruption and treat, and settled back on the couch to watch Green Wing. It's a British show, hospital drama/comedy, emphasis on the comedy. Just what I needed.

Even with Dad still standing over me like he wasn't sure what to do, and Mom pretending to enjoy my TV show, I still wouldn't have rather been anyplace in the world the night before the SATs.

Well, except for maybe in a hot tub with a daiquiri and

fill in the appropriate Hollywood stud here massaging
my shoulders.

Someday.

I dreamed that I went to the bathroom and had a baby.

That I went to the SATs and realized I was fat, too fat to fit behind the desk, because I was pregnant.

That I had to drop out of school and stay at home and take care of a baby.

That Suze was taking a test and crying while a pool of blood formed under her chair.

One thing about the SATs is that it sort of breaks down the barriers of those who take it. No matter how rich or poor your parents are, you still have to take them in the same testing centers, with the same fluorescent lights, same gray wall-to-wall, and same slightly off smell. Groups of dissimilar people huddled around in corners, staring at their feet and laughing nervously. I had taken two of my latest Ritalin haul and was feeling pretty good, last night's nightmare vanishing with the good left-brainy high and tang of sharpened Number 2 pencils in the air.

Suze wasn't taking it until November, so I hung with Lida and her friends—it might have been the first time since he'd traded me the joint for Ritalin that I had seen Dave outside of school, unstoned. He was even dressed okay, polo and jeans, and didn't seem uncomfortable in them.

"This is going to blow," he said amiably, jittering his fingers somewhere between his face and waist. Apparently he was a nicotine freak, too. I guess I never paid attention to all the different types of things he smoked.

"No problem," Lida said, waving her hand down. She had halfheartedly gone through one Kaplan book, then made little designs in the multiple-choice bubbles, claiming it was a design for a hemp bracelet (she never wound up making one).

"'No problem,'" he repeated with a humorless smile, giving Lida a look I thought was only my prerogative. "Easy for you to say. You fail and your dad buys you a spot in Bennington. Or a shop. Or a string of shops."

"A whole goddamn mall, baby," she said, grinning. "And you're forgetting his legacy at Haaaaaaahvad. Besides, I think I really want to go into the music business, and you don't need an Ivy League degree for that."

"Music business? This is new," I said, surprised. "I thought the market for Swedish stoner rock was shrinking."

"Oh no, baby, I'm way past that. Pass the crunk juice, I'm getting into soul."

Dave just shook his head. "Oh Christ, look who's coming," he muttered.

Genevieve was actually *hurrying*. Toward *me*.

"I haven't had a chance to thank you," she said breathlessly, pulling me away from the others. She had a grin from ear to ear with the most beautiful, perfect, pearly white teeth you could imagine, radiating happiness. "Those pills were *amazing*."

"Yeah?" I said, genuinely curious. I had kind of forgotten about her after my depression and subsequent Ritalin re-acquisition.

"I don't have any problems talking to anyone, or at my interviews, or anything," she told me excitedly. "Or at school, or doing my oral reports—or *anything*. It's like I can just leave my bedroom and not fear anyone!"

This was an interesting insight into the Hidden World of Genevieve DeLancie. How many of her friends knew about the beautiful girl who hid in her room, terrified of speaking to her adoring fans?

Not that I really cared right then. The SATs were five minutes away, I was high on Ritalin, and just found her confession a little freakish.

"I'm happy for you." I really was. A little. I just hoped we weren't applying to the same schools. Who asked for photographs.

"I'm even throwing a huge *party* tonight," she said. "Everybody's invited. You should totally come!"

"Thanks, I think I will." All other parties would have probably been pre-empted by this one, except for the mega-partyers—and that was a different crowd.

"Here." She dug into her purse and pulled out a half-full prescription bottle of Ritalin. "Take the whole thing. But you've got to promise to get me more."

"Uh, sure," I said, slipping the bottle into my own bag as quickly as possible. Kind of not the smartest time or place, considering the number of adults watching specifically for cheaters and performance enhancers. Then again, no one would have suspected Genevieve. Or me.

"Promise?" she asked again, uncertainly, looking me in the eye.

"Sure," I said again. Then the bell rang.

I'm not going to bore you with what taking the test itself was like. You probably already know: long, tense, alternately hot and cold, and ultimately just a lot of boring, hard work. A surprising number of questions were almost exactly the same as on the practice tests and then it just became a question of how fast you could fill in the little bubbles. My hand cramped. My fingers reeked of pencil lead and sweat. I lost my concentration exactly once, when someone had a sneezing fit. I looked up but didn't catch the perpetrator, seeing Meera instead, who was sort of staring out into space and tapping her pencil. I think she felt my eyes on her and turned, giving a little smile and wave past the dozens of heads between us, blond and brown and bent down over their silent scribbles.

I almost laughed, but went back to work, grinning instead.

As soon as it was over I stood, stretched, congratulated the people on either side of me, and began the slow shuffle out, watching the strange pairings that only occur in this kind of crucible. A partyer was actually talking about one of the math problems with Kevin, and a rich kid was shaking her head gravely at something Dorianne was saying. Weird.

I was shaky like I had just given birth or something (oog—bad metaphor), but elated, and felt the need to go out and celebrate *now*. In this dizzy state I sought out Will, who was still sitting in his seat, sort of holding court with a few other people, tapping his Number 2 lightly on his knee. He was never still, a possible symptom of ADHD—and a thousand other things, including boredom and nervousness. When he turned and saw me, his gaze was steady and eyes calm.

"Hey," I said cheerfully. "Want to go do something to celebrate?"

"Sure," he said without a moment's hesitation. See, it was things like that which made me think maybe he really did like me back. ("Like me back." Man, that sounds retarded.) "What do you want to do?"

I . . . didn't have any ideas. I opened my mouth, hoping something fun, cool, and appealing would come out. Instead, any hope was shattered when my name was called out ringingly and maternally from the top of the lecture hall.

"Thyme!"

Yeah, it was my mom, practically running down the ramp. I felt my mouth do something funny, a false grin, and just thanked God that she had arrived after almost everyone else had filed out into the hallway.

"Hello, Will," she said, nodding at him.

"Mrs. Gilcrest," Will said right back.

"Hey, I just thought I would come and pick Thyme up myself so we could celebrate. You deserve it," she added, beaming at me.

Great. My last best attempt at actually asking Will out (okay, really "first" and "lamest"), and some radio prompting from Mother Ship suddenly made my mom decide to pick me up to "do something fun" after.

"What kind of fun?" I asked suspiciously.

"My mom took me for ice cream when my tests were done," she said hopefully.

I looked down at Will, maybe for help.

She swooped in for the kill.

"Come with us, Will—it'll be fun!"

So fun that fun was practically being pushed out of her pores. Later I would find out that Mom was on *absolutely nothing* at the time. No mother's little helper, no Valium, no Paxil, no whatever. She was really just trying to bond with her daughter and her friends. And to be fair, that must have taken some effort. She only sort of tolerated Will as my friend—kind of like Lida.

"That sounds great, Mrs. Gilcrest," he said politely, getting up. "Thank you."

On our way out of the lecture hall he opened the door for her without any drama and asked about her job like

he really cared. Unlike, let me think, anyone else I knew,
many of whom called their own parents by their first names.

"What about your other friends?" Mom asked loudly, pointing. Lida was nowhere to be seen, gone the moment the test was over. Who was she pointing at . . . ?

Meera had a piece of paper up against the wall and was writing out something, explaining an answer to another girl, who nodded and left, grimacing to herself.

Oh God, no, I prayed.

"Hey, Meera," Mom called brightly. "We're getting ice cream. You should come! You all haven't hung out together in so long."

And then Science Fiction Freak did something that made me feel really bad. Knowing exactly what her place was in the social strata, Meera looked over at me, letting me know that she completely understood if I said no, that she would wait to hear what I said before accepting.

Well, Suze had flaked on signing up for the test and Lida had gone off with her stoner—or was it raver?—friends and maybe just this once it wouldn't be so bad. There was that huge party tonight—I could afford a little more wacky family and friends time today. And she might provide a nice cushion between Mom and Will (and me).

Giggling a little, Meera and I climbed into the back of my mom's SUV (I let Will have the front seat). It was like Girl Scouts or some other club where you wind up carpooling with kids you don't normally hang with. But there was ice cream at the end of this, not crappy songs and idiotic crafts.

At Wall's we sat at the long, curving counter at the apex (ha! SAT word) of its oxbow (am I pushing it here?).

"So are you all going to Genevieve's party tonight?" I asked, trying to be the good hostess and stimulate conversation between three of the most different people in the senior class (and my mom). I sorta thought movies and music would be right out.

"Can anyone crash?" Will asked, almost interested.

"Is there going to be alcohol there?" Mom asked, definitely interested.

"Yes, and no," I said, pointing to the first and then the second questioner.

"Yeah, I could blow off some steam," Will said, shrugging, reading the menu like it was the *New York Times*.

"There's not going to be alcohol there," Mom stated, extremely dubiously.

"Well, there might be some," I said, trying to sound grudging, "but it's just supposed to be a barbecue, and her parents are going to be there."

It wasn't a total lie if I didn't know what the truth actually was.

"I think I'll probably give it a pass," Meera said, trying to sound adult.

We *all* stared at her. Even Mom.

"There's a *Stargate* marathon on tonight . . . ," she admitted feebly, blushing almost to the color of her freckles (mousy reddish brown, like her hair. Did I ever mention that?).

"Jesus H. Christ, Meera, TiVo the damn thing if it's so important," Will said, exasperated.

"William," my mother warned.

"Sorry, Mrs. Gilcrest. But really, Meer!"

"Meer"? I'm sorry, were these two somehow friends in some other venue and I missed it? I mean, they were neighbors and all, but really. . . .

The nickname in question hunched down in front of her water glass and began stirring the ice with her finger. "I don't know. . . ."

"Come on," Will said, encouraging. "*I'm* going, and I usually avoid these things too."

"This is your senior year, Meera," Mom chimed in unexpectedly. "Real life. Not TV. Have some fun—and keep an eye on these others for me." She indicated me—and maybe Will. Even though I resented the implication, I couldn't help preening a little, being considered a couple at all with him. Even by Mom.

"Maybe," Meera said grudgingly. But I knew that maybe. It was exactly the same sort of maybe that Suze gave Tommy Halder right before they wound up on a bathroom floor together.

"That's the spirit," Will said, clapping her on the back. I watched very closely, but there was nothing untoward about it; he removed his hand instantly and went back to reading the menu.

When the fountain girl came over—yes, in a little paper hat—Meera steeled herself and ordered (somewhat defensively): "I'll have a three-scoop sundae: Peanut Butter Cup, peppermint stick, and orange sorbet, with hot fudge and hot peanut sauce. No whipped cream. No cherry."

The fountain girl looked horrified. Will made a gagging sound.

I laughed out loud. For the first time in, oh, I don't know how long. It was really stupid: my sort-of-date gone completely wrong with one of the biggest freaks of the senior class and the female half of Them, but I was actually having fun. Yeah yeah, without drugs or beer or anything.

But that's the problem, isn't it? If you could bottle moments like that, no one would need to drink, or do Ecstasy . . . or anything else.

14

Bouncing off the Walls

Mommy and Daddy's got the best cocaine
Ritalin's never gonna feel the same
                              —Sugarcult

. . . **Which is why** there was a lot of the above at Genevieve's house that night (and no parents anywhere. They were in Manhattan, or the guest house, to give their girl a little privacy. They must have been thrilled she was finally getting social—her gay older brother was a real debutante, written up on Page Six even before he got into Yale).

The party was supposed to start at eight, which is why I showed up at eleven, though I was planning closer to ten thirty. Suze was, of course, late—*insert menstrual joke here.*

The house was packed with people from a surprising number of different social circles. No one was going to miss something thrown by Genevieve, the hottest smart girl in the school. Well, no one who wasn't invited to one of the Lewis Prep parties.

There was a table set up in the corner with top-shelf liquor and neat stacks of glasses; another in the corner with gift booze: cheap beer, expensive beer, malt beverages, flavored wine, cheap champagne—the usual high school fare. I had brought a bottle of the "cheap" vodka Mom and Dad never drank, a gift from some guest (and gossiped about in the Gilcrest household for weeks after).

Genevieve screamed when she saw me, fighting her way through the crowds and throwing her arms around my shoulders. "Look at this, look at *this!*" she hissed into my ear. She was wearing a party frock that could have been from the sixties and sported matching thick mascara and liner. "This is the party of the season. And it's all thanks to Paxil!"

And *I* sound like a drug ad?

She swung her gaze slowly back at me; her eyes were doe-i-er than usual, a corporate housewife party-throwing dimness that went well with the rest of her mod outfit.

"You're not just on Paxil, are you," I guessed.

She grinned, sparkle-toothed, and gave me a big smack on the cheek, then spun out to talk to other guests.

I put my bottle on the guest table and headed to the top-shelf stuff, making myself a Cosmopolitan, complete with lime twist. Genevieve, the newly perfect hostess, had thoughtfully provided a whole assortment

of garnishes.

Then I felt naked.

None of my friends were there yet—not even Meera. Or Will. Everyone already had a group going on, and yeah, I was terrified of starting up a conversation the wrong way. Being in The Twenty may assure entrance to a good school, but it wins you no social status at a party.

I chugged the Cosmo and made myself another one to sip so I looked cool while I walked around. Idiot girl: I should have started with something harder and faster to bolster my ego.

Finally I headed to the bathroom, because it was a destination and people would think I was going somewhere, not just wandering. I smiled and said hey to everyone as I passed but didn't pause to talk; that would ruin the disguise (and what if they didn't want to talk? What if they were just being polite in saying hi to me?).

The bathroom was gorgeous, with warmed stone floor tiles and a dim glowing light that made *me* look gorgeous when I looked into the mirror. I adjusted my outfit (cream camisole over jeans with a slight silvery tinge to them, might have been sexy on someone else. Yeah, yeah, I know; self-esteem issues. Add it to the list of why I *should* be seeing a therapist) and ran some water to make it sound like I was doing something. Then I noticed a small pile of faint white powdery substance on the marble counter, like someone had been literally powdering her nose.

Now, coke is something I would never in a million years consider doing, but there was very little of it and I was bored and nervous and it was free. I ran my fingertip through it and rubbed it on my gums, following it with my tongue.

Bam.

So much faster than Ritalin.

Right there. Right *there*. I felt good almost instantly, not like a top of the world, snorted-the-Ritalin sort of thing, but solid, confident, and a little giddy.

Totally party.

I went back out into the party and began reintroducing myself to old acquaintances.

Overheard at Genevieve's:

"Did you hear about what happened over in Handon—at the middle school?"

"No, *what?*"

"This kid, he got ahold of his dad's Vicodin prescription or something and handed them out like candy. Like, twenty fifth graders had to be hauled to the hospital."

"No way!"

"*Way.*"

"Here." Lida swirled around me at one point and put something into my hand (how did *she* hear about the party?). "It's Dutch. Totally pure." She was laughing and wearing someone else's glasses, way too big and thick, but somehow they made her look less like a stoner and more like a sexy librarian. It was kind of impressive. I opened my hand and saw a chalky blue tablet sitting there, glistening slightly from my palm sweat. The Calvin Klein logo was pressed into one side.

Before I could say anything, she had twirled away back into the crowd, laughing and kissing some random guy on the cheek, who looked surprised—and then pleased.

And yet, after an hour or two of having really great conversations with people I hadn't talked to since the summer and promising to totally stay better in contact and do go out sometime, I found myself trying to drift back to the people I knew. Watching Suze drink like a fish knowing what was in her belly made me uneasy— even though it would all be fixed soon. There was a room of stoners so thick with smoke I couldn't even see if Lida had wound up there. In the corner, people were either doing yoga or making out, it was hard to tell. Only one person was clearly doing a downward dog.

So guess where I wound up. No, really. *Guess.*

Perched on the edge of a lovely oversize Italian leather daybed populated by, yeah, you win, The Twenty.

They had sort of aggregated around the

entertainment center, the sticky nucleus of which was a giant flat-screen TV and at least three different kinds of console games. Dave and Meera were playing, and Will—*Will!*—was waiting for a turn. Dorianne was fiddling with what looked like an actual key-tar from the eighties and giving advice to the players.

"Over there—to your left! There's a health potion. Down—down—yeah, you got it!"

"I heard Brown won't accept you with a score less than 2100," someone was saying nervously. I didn't recognize her—she wasn't from Ashbury, and wore a tennis dress. Who wears a *tennis* dress to a party?

"Yeah, but who the hell is applying to Brown?" Kevin asked with derision. "They don't even have a business or law school."

I thought of all the beautiful people in all of the different rooms, the ringing laughter, the hooking up upstairs, the talk of yachts and summer trips and other hobbies that didn't involve school. Why was I here? Why was I stuck with these people? Why did I keep coming back and back again? I watched Dave pilot what looked like a paper airplane around a pixelated corner, wishing for some hand-eye and desire. I'm mad skilled at spider solitaire and used to be good at some of the driving games, but that was it. Meera, hopeless loner, had a niche she was enjoying.

"I think I probably got at least a 2100," Tennis Dress Girl said, chewing on her fingernail and chasing it with

a shot of Sambuca. "That's all right, isn't it? With a 3.9
grade point?"

"Did you hear that Casey is actually applying to
Hampshire?" Kevin asked, showing his little bitch colors
after only a few drinks.

"What's wrong with Hampshire?" I asked, truly igno-
rant. I knew it was a little flaky, but that was all.

"*No grades,*" someone said in a hushed voice.

No grades . . . ? I had this vision of a golden paradise,
of happy hippie students sitting around on porches discussing philosophy and medical ethics, while a warm
late-afternoon sun shone down on a small patch of lov-
ingly tended organic tomatoes and weed.

"Just written evaluations. It's total bullshit," Kevin
said, throwing a shot back down his throat. Something
green and rank looking, like from *Star Trek*. "Like business schools and recruiters are going to give a rat's ass
about your social development."

"What have you heard about Brandeis?" Hal Pelling
(our basketball star and GPA #13) asked nervously. "Do
big companies like *them*?"

"Will you people just fucking shut up already?" Will
suddenly yelled. Loudly. Very loudly. The conversations
in the other rooms lulled.

But he didn't care.

"Holy Christ," Will swore, putting his drink down.
"Why do any of you even bother with all of this? You
cram and study and volunteer to teach orphaned

dolphins how to dance just to get into snotty colleges so you can graduate, become consultants, get married, and raise little clones . . . who you force to do flash cards, cram, and study all over again. None of you is going to be a Nobel Prize winner or cure cancer or write poetry. So what the hell's the point?"

An explosion or lightbulb went off in my head.

That was it.

I was angry all the time about the future I didn't want with people I didn't like. But I didn't know what I wanted—so what else was there to do? That one path seemed unavoidable.

"You don't know what you're talking about," one girl (GPA #8) said with a disdainful slur.

"Yeah? Are you going to cure cancer?" he shoved his face into hers. "Or are you going to become vice president at some insurance company for ten years before you drop out and start having babies?"

"Will," Kevin said with what was supposed to be, I guess, a warning tone.

Will just rolled his eyes and stood up. "I'm out of here."

He stalked out with the grim dignity of someone who really couldn't care less if everyone he left behind suddenly had their heads explode.

"I *love* that guy," Dave said, pulling out a cigarette.

"Amen," Meera muttered.

I ran out after him.

"Wait! Will!"

It was a replay of the party that summer, except that I was running after him, we were all an academic year older, it was chillier out, and people in the yard—making a bonfire—were watching.

Will turned around. "Yeah?"

"Is *that* what you think of me?" I demanded. "Is that why you don't want to hang out with me or go out with me or anything? Because you think I'm like all those other people? Kevin? Genevieve? The people you hate?"

"What are you talking about?" he asked, now a little unsure, but still seething.

"Do you really think I'm like all those other people?" I demanded, slowly and carefully.

Because I hated them. Holy Christ, as Will would say, I hated them. I hated them and Them and sometimes Suze and Lida but more than anything else in the world I hated them. And being one of them. I had never realized just how much.

"No, Gilcrest," he said uneasily. "You're not like those jerks in there at all. I don't understand why you're always trying to be friends with them."

"Then why won't you hang out with me?" I asked, trying not to cry, trying not to feel like an idiot, trying not to imagine everyone in the front yard staring at us from behind their bonfire like cavemen.

Will smiled crookedly. "Uh, up until today, you've never really asked."

"What?"

He couldn't be that stupid. No one could be that stupid. Could they?

He shrugged. "You always ask me *the day after* why I wasn't someplace, or tell me how great a movie was and how I should have been there, so . . . I don't know. I just assumed if you'd wanted me there you would have asked, instead of giving me the play-by-play like I was your Sensitive Male Friend."

I rubbed my hand over my face in exhaustion.

"It's been a long day," I finally said, feeling it—getting up at seven, six hours of testing, a whole ice-cream sundae, and a four-hour party come crashing down on my shoulders. "Would you walk me home?"

Will grinned.

"Absolutely." He put out his hand and I took it, marveling immediately how its warmth and touch seemed to take about a million of the aforesaid pounds off my back. "What about your friends?"

I thought about Lida, who may or may not have been in the stoner room, and Suze, who was probably contemplating—if not already in—a soccer player sandwich.

"Fuck 'em," I said, grinning back.

Name	Patient's Comment	Diagnosis	Preferred Prescription	Notes
David	Wants to remain "comfortably numb"	Stoner	Um, der	Note the complete lack of Ritalin/weed crossover.
Dorianne	"I'm so depressed. . . ."	Bipolar depressant	Celexa/Lexapro Try Depakote? Zoloft?	
Kevin	"I'm a little bitch."	Complete ass. Okay, really: Type-A anxiety type	Valium	Not too much. Guy has the metabolism of a five-year-old girl
Genevieve	Needs to "dial down the pressure"	Social anxiety disorder	Zanies short term, Paxil long	Can get Adderall
Sonia Lansing	???? Kind of quiet this year			Can get daddy's Vicodin
Hal Pelling	Jock/Stealth Twenty?!?!	ADD	Adderall	Diagnosed w/ ADHD for five years
~~Frederick Groven~~		~~Needs a fucking life~~		~~$$$ Ritalin~~ Screw him
Dave Underwood		ADHD	Ritalin	
Renny Manning		ADHD	Concerta	
Michael Lowingbrook		ADHD, generalized anxiety disorder	Adderall/ Strattera	
Jun Kim		Full-time partyer	Vitamin R and Adderall (ingested nasally) Harder stuff (e, etc.)	THROWS THE BEST PARTIES!!! GET INVITED!

15

Station to Station

It's not the side effects of the cocaine
I'm thinking that it must be love
                              -David Bowie

Ah, November.

If October was my month of trying to change things,
of proaction, of getting shit done, November was a time to
tie loose ends, follow up on things, work out the details. A
lot of which involved updating my database. Even those
who took their pills on a regular basis would occasionally jump at the chance to earn a quick untraceable
twenty (and, as my confidence grew, it was easier to
talk to them). Who doesn't like a sudden free CD, dinner
at Nerina's, or an extra four hundred messages for their
cell phone? Not Dave Underwood, Renny Manning, or
Michael Lowingbrook, that's for sure.

November was also the month by which all the early
applicants had to early applicant. Fill out their forms,

request financial aid (giggle), and get interviewed by
local alums.

I think the amount of antianxiety drugs in the collective systems of Ashbury's senior overachievers could have poisoned a large pond. Kevin came to me for extra Valium, and most of The Twenty came by at one time or another for whatever I had to offer.

To keep up with demand I actually volunteered to go over to Cassandra's house with Mom so I could go through her medicine cabinets. I now did this at all of my parents' friends' houses—who didn't have a kid at Ashbury. As they say on those nature shows, don't piss where you drink.

I wound up selling the Ecstasy Lida gave me for less than what it was really worth—but made an investment in the future.

"Hey." I approached Jun (the present leader of the partyers) in the hall, looking annoyed and put out. "I know you've got a party coming up and I need to get rid of this—my parents are doing the we-don't-trust-our-daughter thing this week, so there's a forecast of rain with a major chance of snooping in my near future."

Nice, huh? I'd practiced it in front of a mirror.

The pill was in a little dimebag I normally used for beads—I waved it gently at him.

He raised one eyebrow. I don't know what it is about me and eyebrows, but they're just so darn sexy when used properly.

"Why don't you just take it?"

"Because I'm allergic to Ketamine," I said facetiously. "And I have no idea if this is a real CK or not."

Yeah, I know Lida said it was pure. *Lida*. Think about it.

(Oh, and for those of you out of the know, let me explain: Besides all the *usual* dangerous effects and side effects of drugs, illegal ones are often cut with *other* substances—sometimes illegal, to enhance the high, sometimes toxic, as a filler. Just a heads-up.)

Jun laughed. "I had no idea you were such a connoisseur." His eyes flicked over me as if rescanning my image, replacing whatever information was in his mental database previously. I honestly couldn't tell if the new Thyme was a possible sex object, similar partyer, or some combination of the two. I tried to look bored. "Okay, I'll give you ten."

If I told him it was really Dutch, like it was supposed to be, I probably could have gotten twenty. Ah, well.

He opened his Coach wallet and pulled a crisp ten out of a neat wad of twenties. It took me a moment to realize what was strange about what I was seeing, before it finally hit me: the amount of cash he had. No one I knew carried that much. Like I said, everything was credit card, and mostly paid for by Mommy and Daddy. Even the "poorer" kids didn't carry much more than lunch money around.

Question: Why would a student have so much cash on him?

Answer: to buy things not for sale by credit card. Or

to show off.

Or, much like his new estimation of me, some combination thereof.

"Thanks," I said, shoving it in my own purse like it wasn't really worth anything to me (a few Ritalin).

"Where'd you get it?" he asked, trying to sound casual.

I shrugged. "Around."

He smiled. "Can you get more?"

I smiled back. "Oh, probably."

"You should come to one of my parties sometime," he finally suggested, meaning it.

Bingo. My work here was done. I was finally going to the Big Cool Parties: no members of The Twenty invited, thank you. No discussions of grades, no verbal competition, no mention of College and Career; just fun and fun people and gorgeous people and fun.

And I didn't have to ask. *He* asked me.

His smile was divine. If he had grabbed me and kissed me then I probably wouldn't have let go for an hour or two. It wasn't just his looks, it was his aura. Everything around him seemed exciting.

"Yeah, I'd like that," I said, trying not to grin.

And speaking of not speaking of college, for those of us *not* applying early it was time to get seriously down to our applications. Age, name, rank, serial number, favorite hobbies, favorite classes, favorite books, extra-currics, and what you think *A Dream Deferred* is really about. At least *that* question had a focus. Frigging Dartmouth wanted me to ask my own question and answer it. I got clever, probably a bad idea, and asked myself what I would do if I didn't go to college.

That was the only fun I had with the entire process, actually planning out two or four years of life in a dream world.

Yes, I would travel. Yes, I would waste time on a beach somewhere. Maybe I would even try to sell my beaded jewelry. I've never had a job—Mom and Dad didn't want it to interfere with schoolwork. I've never earned any money, had to support myself, or learned how to cook. I would do all those things. Yes, and party—who doesn't want to party. I would get a crap-ass apartment somewhere in Venice, California, and work retail during the day and sell my jewelry at night and the weather would be in the eighties year round, sunny, and I would barely get by and later I would remember those days for the rest of my life.

"Aw *frick!*" Suze swore, throwing some important application document down on my bed harder than was strictly necessary—and interrupting my train of thought. She began to shuffle through the rest of her scattered papers like a raccoon looking for tasty bits of garbage. "Where did page six go?"

"You, uh," I cleared my throat gently. "You're going to have to get a little better organized there, Kemosabe."

My hands paused over the keyboard like a, I don't
know, *butterfly* hovering over a flower, unsure whether
to stay in the air or land (do they even do that?). For a
couple minutes there I had been far away from this world
and deep into another, almost not caring about the application itself. Was it all gone? I closed my eyes and tried to
conjure images of foamy waves and crystal beads and
breakfast burritos.

"Did you hear about Meera?" Suze asked brightly,
changing the subject to something more interesting, less
about her.

"I noticed she was out today." I shrugged, squinting at
the screen, hoping that the appearance of concentration
would lead to actual concentration.

"She broke her leg on a skiing trip with her dad in
Aspen. Can you believe it! At the beginning of the season and everything!"

"How horrible," I said, meaning it. As soon as I was
done with this essay I would send her a card or something. I had no idea Meera did anything as cool as skiing.

"Apparently the bone was *sticking through her
skin*," Suze said, leaning forward and stage-whispering.
"They gave her all sorts of stuff, Vicodin and OxyContin,
but she wouldn't take it. Only Tylenol."

I wasn't surprised, given her little lecture in the locker
room that day about "managing your cramps."

"There's a fucking waste," Lida muttered. She wasn't
really working on her applications, either, choosing instead

to poke around my bureau—my *private* drawers—looking for something sparkly. She had managed to concentrate on her applications for exactly one half hour before getting bored and restless. "Hey, got any new creations? Earrings or bracelets or something in pink? I'm trying to match this wild pair of pants I just got."

"I haven't made anything in a while," I said, trying not to snap. They were like a fricking pair of monkeys. If someone had left a pile of poo out on the floor Suze and Lida would have been flinging it at each other by now. "Look, I thought we were all supposed to support each other tonight. Get through some of this shit."

"Yeah, yeah. Hey, these are cool—can I borrow these?" Lida pulled out a pair of earrings I'd made a lo-ong time ago. Gold-filled wire with little aquamarine-colored Swarovski crystals. A little Bollywood, a little rock 'n' roll.

"Um, sure, whatever." I ran my hand through my hair. That would probably be the last I ever saw of those, and I kind of liked them.

"Hey, Suze, what do you think?" she said, spinning around and holding them up to her ears.

"Oh my God, with a scarf around your head they would look *great*," Suze agreed.

"I'm going to go put them on." Lida ran off to the bathroom. Not really sure why, there was a mirror on my bureau.

I turned back to the computer screen, empty-headed.

I switched over to my mail program and, strapped for anything else to do, e-mailed Will. He didn't IM.

Hey. Want—to—go—to—a—movie?
—Thyme

The answer came back almost instantly.

Nothing good out. I have a better idea. What are you doing the day before Thanksgiving?

Well, probably going to a pre-TG party, or one of the pre-Black Friday sales, or hanging out at home listening to my parents bitch about going to Grandma and Grandpa's.

Nothing really, I responded.

No "instant" message back this time.

I sighed and got up. Lida was still in the bathroom and Suze was frowning with great concentration at one of the forms. *Wesleyan*.

"Hey," I said gently, sitting at the edge of the bed. It was time to address the biggest loose end of the fall so far, one that should be tied up quickly. "We should probably think about getting you to the doctor, soon."

"What?" Suze asked, distracted, still staring at the paper.

"The doctor? For your—uh—" What did they call it in the movies and TV? What was synonymous and acceptable? *"Procedure?"* I rubbed my belly to indicate what kind.

"Oh, that. I don't need it anymore," she said, shrugging and putting the paper aside, picking up another one. "I started bleeding right after Genevieve's party. False alarm."

I think my relief lasted maybe all of four seconds. It would come back later that night, when I was lying in bed, replaying the dread and horror of the situation for the last couple of weeks, imagining how I would have felt if I was her. For now, however, it was replaced by a shooting geyser of anger.

"After the *party*? A few *weeks* ago?" I demanded, trying to remain calm. But my voice shook.

"What?" She looked up, then saw my face and was instantly contrite. "Oh, I'm sorry. I totally should have told you. You've been so great to me throughout all this." She leaned forward and hugged me. "I just, I don't know, when it happened, never wanted to think about it again."

I wish I could say I understood. I didn't. I sat there and let her hug me and quietly wished her head would explode.

"Okay, what's the surprise?"

My breath came out with little puffs of steam, like old-fashioned trains once might have at the very Metro-North station we were meeting at. The sky was a clear, bright winter blue, and everything seemed crystal and icy. I wore my "Little Red Riding Hood" coat, dark red angora and wool, oversize gray cashmere mittens and earmuffs that made me look, well, adorable.

Will was wearing a really nice shiny black leather jacket and an aviator scarf, accessorized with a digital camera cunningly disguised to look like an old-fashioned one. He could have been either the photographer at a fashion shoot or a model pretending to be a photographer in a fashion shoot. Well, his legs were a little short to be a real model. But you get the idea.

Really fricking hot.

I don't know what happened to him this past summer, but he went from grunge to decked out as gracefully as an ice skater coming out of a triple axel.

I only use that metaphor because I thought maybe we were going ice skating. Every winter at the club they set up a little log cabin near the pond and sell really incredible hot cocoa and rent skates and keep the ice clear of snow. Sometimes they even have a DJ at night. Like most New Englanders, I can definitely hold my own on blades. And Will used to do ice hockey, so I figured . . .

"Come on, let's get on," he said, pointing at the westbound train that was about to leave.

"Uh." I stopped. "Where are we going? I'm not supposed to go to the city without telling Mom and Dad, and—"

"Oh, for Christ's sake, Gilcrest," Will said, rolling his eyes. "How old are you, twelve? *I'm* supposed to be at an SAT retake course. Come on."

He took me by the hand again and led me forward.

"Why are we taking the train?" I demanded, whining. Sitting shotgun next to him in that giant boat of a car his parents owned would have been fun. We could have put some music on, turned the bass up . . . "Why can't you drive?"

"What, global warming happening too slowly for you? Besides, the car would be missed." He ran as the speakers began to blare something incomprehensible, electronic mutterings about a train leaving, a train arriving, or the end of the world. We ran up the platform and with a mighty sprint barely made it inside, Will holding the door for me as it beeped and banged, wanting to close.

I laughed—second time recently, second time with Will. I almost felt giddy. No, correct that, I *did* feel giddy.

"So where are we going?" I said again in a whiny voice, after we found seats on the south side of the car so we could watch the coast speed by.

"You'll see," he said with that annoying smile of his. "Something I've always wanted to do."

I figured it would be cheesy, like the Empire State Building, but what the hell, I hadn't done it since I was a kid, and it was definitely romantic.

The forty-five-minute ride flew: We talked about *everything*. Music and movies and school and then religion and friends and parents and the government and war.

But he *still* wouldn't tell me what we were doing, not even on the subway from Grand Central to Central Park Something (I was impressed at his knowledge; every time I come here with friends we just take cabs). I hadn't quite lost hope yet that it was skating. When I was little, every year we would go at Christmas, once at Rock Center and once at Wollman Rink in the Park. Rock Center was way more glamorous, but if you tripped, people from all over the world, NBC and CBS and Time Warner, saw you.

It was really cold. Colder than in Ashbury, it seemed like. He lead us through many strange paths in faux woods where I was sure we were going to get raped or something, too worried to fully enjoy it. We finally came to a rock at the edge of a clearing and he pulled me forward, shouting: ta-dah!

At first I had no idea what I was looking at. Giant, colorful slugs undulated slowly over the landscape like an apocalypse in New York, Japanese animation style. Closer inspection revealed scores of ministering humans running back and forth with ropes and shouts. Underneath it all there was a low rumbling, like a wind through a tunnel.

Will grinned. "They're blowing up the floats for the Macy's parade tomorrow."

Suddenly the picture reset itself and I understood what I was looking at: In the far corner of the field there was a giant black-and-white Mickey Mouse. Closer, something that looked suspiciously like Superman still hugged the ground flatly—only the S on his chest gave it away. "I've always wanted to come see it and take pictures, but I never wanted to do it by myself."

Before I started devoting myself to getting into college 24/7, yes, I did date. And no, I had never been on one anything like this.

I was grinning too. He waited until *me* to do this. ME!

This kicked a dinner at Tavern on the Green right on its ass.

He took my hand, and like a pair of kids in a fairy tale, we went down into the valley of the Half-Inflated Floats.

And in the half-light of the train on the way back, after some nice panning-to-the-sky time, I fell asleep against his shoulder.

16

Thanksgiving
(No Way Out)

I feel a closing in
Living this way

—Violent Femmes

Over the river and through the woods.

I took a bunch of books in the back of the car with me on the way to Grandma and Grandpa's so I could refamiliarize myself with My Favorite Books (hint: they're not actually my favorite books. Can you say *college application?*). *A Separate Peace* and *The Catcher in the Rye* were just too obvious, *Anna Karenina* too unlikely, and besides, I hadn't read it. *Fight Club* would be more honest, but how many other teens would claim it? *Pride and Prejudice* was possible, but *Perks of Being a Wallflower* had more appeal. Nonfiction might be a better option, though: unusual and inspiring. I brought along a couple of biographies, including the one about that climber guy who lost his arm. Poetry was right out. I can't lie that well.

My *actual* favorite book is probably this old, generic beading book from the eighties that is just encyclopedic. Anything I ever suddenly needed to know—how to close a leather thong with a crimp clasp, how to do a peyote stitch, how to dab glue exactly where you need it—is in there, along with hundreds of projects that I like to read through when I need comfort, or right before sleep, imagining how I would do it and what it would look like in the end.

Oh, also *Boy Proof*. It's about a kind of a freak, sort of an über-Meera, but she lives in California and knows how to make monster masks out of latex and chooses to intern on a movie set instead of going straight to college.

Not the sort of thing you tell an admissions officer about.

Mom and Dad were in the front seat arguing quietly about money or scheduling—Mom had her check-and-date book out. Say what you will about the advancement of the feminist cause, when They're both in the car together, Dad always drives. Always.

"How are those applications coming along?" he called back.

"Fine," I mumbled.

"I'll look at them when you're done," he offered.

"Thanks, I'm okay."

Dad might have been a veep or whatever, but his writing skills were definitely subpar. At least Mom knew how to punctuate. I always wondered if his work e-mails were lowercase with too many exclamation points, the

way little kids write. I planned on having the guidance counselor and maybe Mrs. Tildenhurst go over my essays with a fine-toothed red pen.

"No, I'll look at them when you're done," he decided. He used that voice that brooked *no* disagreement. Commanding. Domineering. Final. His word was God. It made me itchy, or want to kill him, every time. "This is too important. Take all the help you can get. That's one of the most important rules of the adult world."

I didn't answer.

Mom looked out the window.

"Hey, those are my earrings," I said, noticing the small beaten gold hoops she was wearing. Not my design—strictly Tiffany's.

"I'm sorry, I needed something to go with my necklace. I wouldn't normally go through your dresser, you know that."

"No problem," I said, genuinely unconcerned. Mom fixed me with a weird look that I didn't think about until later, because then she did something *else* weird. Something I never would have noticed before—like those boys around the NyQuil bottle. She reached with one hand into her purse, popped something open, and popped something else into her mouth.

"What was that?" I demanded.

"Breath mint," she said quickly. And didn't offer me one.

Breath mint my ass. Not ten minutes later her eyes

were glassy, but otherwise the interior of the car didn't change its silence.

Actually, except for being alone with Them in the car, I kind of enjoy Thanksgiving. There's the fun of *enduring* the adults with my cousins, and that weird sort of insta-bond you can only get with family, no matter how long it's been since you've seen them.

And there were only a few awkward moments.

"So, Thyme, what are *your* plans?" Grandpa asked in his booming voice, directing his full attention on me.

The words came out of my mouth like they were put there by my zombie master, all those things I told Will I hated. But out they still came.

"I'm applying to Harvard and Dartmouth and Amherst—"

Grandpa snorted. "That last one better be a backup."

"And a few others, planning on a major in economics with a minor in international development."

He nodded, just like those words were meant to make him. Maybe I had it reversed: Maybe *I* was the zombie master, saying these spells that always soothed my listeners, made them nod and take me seriously and then move on, assuaged and pleased by answers they couldn't remember later.

(SAT vocab word-a-day phone call, September 12: *shibboleth*—a word or phrase used to determine if the user is part of a group or an outsider.)

"So are you dating anyone?" Grandma asked,

wielding the giant knife as expertly as Uma did in *Kill Bill*.

"Yeah," I answered without thinking, grabbing a bowl of salad.

Mom made a choking noise.

"What?"

"Sort of," I amended.

"Oh, I didn't mean to ruin the secret," Grandma said with a sly chuckle. Mom went red and matched it with a big slurp of red wine. The boys all chose to laugh heartily at that moment. I felt kind of bad; Grandma was easier to let things slip to than my mom. But I felt like I did an "end around" on her, as Dad would say.

"It's, uh, nothing big. Only been out on, like, one date so far."

"Anyone I know?" Mom asked dryly, swirling her Syrah. My aunt and grandma exchanged a look, and I was embarrassed for—and hateful toward—everyone.

"Will," I said, concentrating on adding some broccoli rabe to the giant stack of food that was looking less and less pleasant to wolf down as I lost my appetite.

"*Will?*" I could sense what was coming next, but there was no way to prevent it. "Wasn't he the one who smashed up that kid's bicycle?"

"Uh, yeah, that was a while ago. He's been in therapy."

"I see."

Apparently he was okay enough to have ice cream with, but not okay enough for a daughter to date. I wondered just how much racism had to do with it. Regardless, later I was going to get the lecture again about not surrounding myself with losers. Or dating them. Fuck. I was such an idiot.

Hours later, when we were all getting our coats and saying our good-byes, my cousin Hauser took me aside.

"So, you got any Valium?" he asked casually, like he was asking for aspirin or a cigarette (or a breath mint).

As a matter of fact, I did. My blinged-up Altoids tin of the good stuff was at home tonight, but I always carried around one or two pills for emergencies (uh, not so much for me. I had my Ritalin supply and dosage under control to the point where I never got heart shakiness anymore. I mean like emergency trades or deals). I dug around in my purse and pulled out a couple.

"Stressed out at school?" I asked, feeling very adult interacting with my cousin on this level.

"What? God, no. No, it's for the ride home. Three hours of being in the backseat goes a lot faster when you spend it with Prince Valium."

Mighty Cousin Hauser, my Nemesis and Idol, began to crumble (in my head).

"You're taking it for boredom?" I asked with no small amount of disgust.

He rolled his eyes and gave a little laugh. "Oh my God, Thyme. You're too much." Then he popped the pills into his mouth and followed it with the rest of the wine,

wandering off to get his coat.

In the backseat of my own car, going home, I thought, Shit, I'm bored too.

But *I* brought books.

While They had a drink to unwind from holiday dinner and drinks with The Family, I went upstairs to go to bed. Tomorrow was Black Friday, and yeah, I always used to go shopping with Suze and Lida. But this year I was thinking of implementing a new tradition: *not*. Lida because she hated everything pretty and decent and fashionable and would spend the entire time stoned or making snarky comments, Suze because her flaking on telling me about her not-pregnant-anymore-ness still pissed me off. They both also sometimes swiped things they wanted—which was funny when we were thirteen, and now was just dead embarrassing (and potentially catastrophic. Rentacops aren't so amusing when they have you by the ear and are phoning your parents).

I went into the drawer in my bureau to take my nightly vitamin R—I hadn't that day—but the Altoids tin was gone.

17

Changes

I had no one to turn to in my panic.

Will was at his grandparents in L.A. for the weekend, and Lida turned out to be sort of AWOL after all. What should have been a kick-ass three-day weekend of shopping, resting, and okay, working on my applications a little, turned into a horrible, lonely game of waiting for the other shoe to drop.

Remember that "weird" look my mom gave me in the car? Right after she said how she wouldn't normally *go through my stuff?*

And besides, who else would take them? Maria, our housekeeper? Shit, if she wanted to steal something to sell, she could have chosen a billion other little things; my mom has so much jewelry she'd never miss anything

for months. It could only have been Them. But when
would They confront me? Why not do it in the car, when
I couldn't escape? What was taking so long? Were They
waiting until all the psychiatrists and intervention coun-
selors were back from holiday? Was Mom taking time to
look up each of the pills on the Internet?

Was the waiting just for torture, part of my punish-
ment?

And, of course, there was the thought that maybe, a
little dopey from the Ambien I had begun to occasionally
pop when I couldn't sleep, I'd put them somewhere else.

I turned my room upside down. Literally. Every little
thing.

When Monday morning came I was as exhausted as
if it were Friday after a week of midterms. If Mom and
Dad were going to pull anything, it would probably be
when they got home from work and I got home from the
Student Council pre-PTA meeting brainstorm session.
Just twelve whole hours of agony.

Fortunately, I finally had Will to distract myself with.
Besides hanging out whenever we could, we were
going on real dates now: an after-school slice at Nerina
and making out at a bench nearby. Walks up and down
autumnal, deserted streets. Movies with the usual crowd
showing up. Movies without the usual crowd showing
up. Things were a little different now that we were hanging out with each other and not, say, with Suze or Dave.

We were treated differently, given a little privacy, given a few props. We were a *couple.*

Not so much with the hanging-out-at-the-mall, though; I hadn't been to the Galleria in forever. Rampant consumerism made Will itchy, and unlike a lot of big talkers at school, he practiced what he preached. I get itchy too when I see nine-year-olds demanding Pottery Barn Kids (and dudes like my dad buying soda machines for their rec rooms branded with their favorite teams). I never had anyone to share that feeling with before.

Will was so cool. I just wished I could have talked to him about what was going on—I was pretty sure he knew about the drugs, but I never drew overt attention to them and he never mentioned anything. They were kind of an open secret.

Like that week, when we were walking down the hall together and I spotted Hal Pelling. He was so much easier to buy from than that idiot drama queen Freddy that I made a big note of it in my spreadsheet later.

"Hey, I'll see you," I said, kissing Will lightly on the cheek as I turned to go.

"What do you want with our basketball star?" Will asked, not so much suspiciously but strangely—like he knew the answer but wanted to hear it aloud, from me.

"Oh, nothing really, just some stuff," I answered airily, but looking him in the eye: *Do you really want to know?*

He looked at me for a long, hard moment, as if he was

going to say something. He said something else instead.
"Just please don't do anything to fuck with this," he said,
pointing at me and him and the space between us. "It's
pretty good."

"I know," I said, kissing him again. Fully aware he
wasn't talking about jealousy or hitting on other guys.

As soon as he was gone down the hall, I turned to Hal.

"Hey, I'm almost out of my own Ritalin. . . ." Which in
its own way was true. "I was wondering . . . ?"

"Oh, uh, sure." He reached into his bag, one of those
hug-your-back-flat ones a lot of kids in the city used.
"Here." He pulled out his prescription bottle—no secrets
here—and carefully tapped out three.

"Can I . . . ?" I opened my wallet.

"Oh, uh, yeah. Let's call it five." He shrugged his tall,
bony shoulders and frowned, which really was his only
expression: seriousness, with that rare faint smile.

Yeah, I know: *While* waiting to find out if They found
my stash or until I found it myself, with all of Authority
and Rules and College Acceptance hanging over my
head as this little mystery played out, I actually *went out
of my way* to buy more? Was I insane? Hadn't I learned
my lesson?

Fair point. But only if you completely missed the part
where I came down hard off of Ritalin. Or the bit where
my test scores went up on it.

"Anytime you need any, let me know," Harold said,
turning away. I wondered if that was his "tell." When he

faced me again it was with that faint smile. "But you have to come to one of our games, promise?"

I was genuinely touched—and amused. Who ever heard of someone dealing drugs in exchange for a sports audience? Then again, he could have gently been hitting on me—but before I could think about it too much, Lida walked by, talking with someone—*not* Dave or Suze—and she was so distracting that it took all of my concentration to finish up the conversation politely.

"What the hell is up with *that*?" I demanded as soon as the lanky basketball player was gone. I grabbed Lida by the shoulder and spun her around to get a good look.

You know those retarded little white-T-shirt-and-pastel-knit-ballet-top things people were wearing for a while? Imagine a dark green top instead, with embroidery and a fringe and beads hanging off of it like seaweed. But it was the pants that stopped me. Big, flowing pink harem pants. And little gold-stamped leather slippers.

What happened to camo stoner chic?

"Yeah, I kept your earrings. Sorry, but they inspired the whole outfit. What do you think?" She pirhouetted en point so I could get the full effect. Damn, but my earrings really did look good with the outfit. The colors in the stones and the almost-paisley-paramecium pattern really brought the whole thing together, colors that would normally clash. Badly.

"Okay, fine, whatever, keep them," I said. "They look great." She was still wearing the thick-rimmed glasses she had picked up at the party and was still using an army bag for books; this was Lida in transition, as if you could peek inside the chrysalis. In just a few more days she would emerge, complete with new personality. "But, uh, what happened to the Shins concert tees and hemp Converses?"

She laughed. The girl next to her, I finally noticed, was Sara Leisel, a devotee of Robert Thurman and in every bleeding heart club at school, mostly Free Tibet.

"Over and *done*." Lida looked unsure for a very flash second. "We need to talk, later." Then she sort of leaned back on her feet and gave me that cocksure smile. "Peace *out*."

As she and her new gal pal wandered off, I just shook my head. At least her phases were less physically harmful than Suze's. Who knows, she might do some good for the world.

All radio lines remained silent.

No matter how many opportunities I gave Them, They didn't say anything.

I quietly rebuilt my inventory and stepped lightly at school.

And in the Hall of Fame for Ironic Things in Thyme's Life, the topic for this week's PTA meeting was . . .

Drug abuse.

Real drugs, not prescription ones. But it still wasn't easy to sit for two hours listening to the local police detective, the head of the PTA, and our principal talk about them. I took dutiful notes. Absolutely positive the entire time someone would whip out my Altoids tin and shake it above everyone's heads as evidence.

The meeting was in one of the conference rooms on the second floor in our school, a sea of Burberry and barn coats for the parents and not-quite-right suits for the teachers. Eau d' cheap coffee permeated everyone.

Maybe if they gave the teachers a proper espresso machine, Mr. Handley's breath wouldn't stink so bad?

I made a note of it.

"I'm worried—and I think rightfully—that someone might offer my teenager drugs, or already has," Concerned Mother #1 piped up. She raised her hand gracefully but strongly, the queen of England in Isotoners.

"Well, ma'am," the detective said politely, "that's why we have these programs, to teach you how to talk to your kids about drugs. The best way to keep them *off* of drugs is to keep communication lines open. And to tell them not to do drugs. Over and over again."

"But shouldn't you be doing a better job keeping drugs out of our schools to begin with? So they're not exposed?" Concerned Mother #2 spoke up, causing #1 to press her lips together irritably—that was going to be *her* follow-up question.

"We're doing all we can, ma'am," the detective said,
trying to remain calm. His features were etched deeply
into his face, although he wasn't that old. Black hair and
black eyes and black lines delineated his cheekbones,
chin, brow. Bags under his eyes. I wished I could draw
like Will. It would make an interesting portrait. "But thinking you can keep your child completely isolated from the
offer, presence, or pressure of drugs is naive in this day
and age. Forget about the lunchroom—do you know
what your kids are doing when they're at each others'
houses, or even home?"

It was a fair point. Mom had vague concerns about
Lida being a stoner almost-dropout loser type without
even realizing Suze was the teen pregnant queen. They
were charmed by her, just like everyone else.

And they thought there might be a "little" alcohol at
the party I went to.

Not lines of coke in the bathroom.

"Yes, yes I do," the woman answered smugly. The
detective just rolled his eyes and looked at the principal
for help.

"What about dogs?" Concerned Father spoke up. "I
heard at another school they had a surprise lockdown
and took drug dogs through the halls and found all sorts
of drugs in the kids' lockers and bags."

Huh, that was interesting.

The other parents must have thought so too; there
were loud mumbles of surprise and approval.

"That's not going to win you any points from your kids," the policeman said, shrugging. "If you want to, we'd be happy to cooperate and help you organize it. But, remember folks, those dogs aren't perfect, and they're only trained for specific things."

"Like what?" Concerned Dad asked.

The detective shrugged again. "Coke, heroine, pot."

More murmurs.

"That sounds fine," a Slightly Less Concerned Dad said aloud. "What else is there?"

Scattered laughter. I tried not to roll my eyes.

"OxyContin," the detective shot back. "Demerol, Percodan, Percocet. *Cough syrup.* More common prescription drugs like Prozac, Xanax, Ritalin, the so-called study drugs . . ."

Oh, look at that, my palms were sweating. Fascinating. I'd have taken something to calm down, if only I had any.

"The prescription drug abuse rate among high school students is *second only to pot.* Everything else—coke, heroin, acid, Ecstasy—they all come in farther down the list. Especially in a town like Ashbury."

Concerned parents muttered among themselves.

"A janitor found this just last week," the detective said, pulling out my Altoids tin.

I was torn between staring and throwing up.

It was missing a few little blings, a couple of rhinestones had fallen off here and there, but it still sparkled gaily in the fluorescent lights.

"It contained over twenty pills—including antidepressants, opiates, uppers, downers—everything
I've mentioned here, *and all perfectly legal.*"

So this was it.

In the next moment the detective—who'd seemed so
tragic before—was going to point at me, shouting, "AND
THERE SHE IS!"

It all made sense. They knew I would be here, and
what a great example it would be for other kids.

In fact, it was the only perfect and logical ending to the
Story of Thyme: academic overachiever resorts to drugs to
keep up, begins to deal to ensure her own supply (and learns
to love the power over her so-called friends), but is finally
brought down at a PTA meeting in front of the entire town.

They wouldn't handcuff me, right? In my panic, I fix-
ated on that one thing. Cops melting out of the crowd
and shackling me before I could cry.

You know how girls don't perspire, they "glow"? *I* was
sweating. I felt it trickle down my spine and pool into my
buttcrack. The only thing that kept me in my seat was
that getting up would be *really fricking obvious.*

"We have no idea whose this is," the detective went
on. "Some dealer, obviously. Probably stolen from the
original owner—it was found in a bathroom trash can.
We'll never know, just like the nickel bag of weed we
found in the smokers' tree behind the school."

Relief flooded my body like Gatorade in one of those
gross ads, blue liquid oozing out pores.

"My point is, this stuff is really happening. With your kids. In this school. Your proof's right here. Pretending it doesn't will not help you fight it."

Honestly, I don't remember most of the meeting after that. A lot of slow, measured breathing, a broken pencil tip, an ulcer popping, a mystery explained, a mystery still unsolved.

And one thought overriding them all: *They are this close to me. It was only a matter of luck I wasn't caught this time.*

Afterward, one of the Concerned Parents saw me with my notepad and gave a nervous chuckle.

"You're not going to report back all of our secret plans, are you?"

A thousand different responses leaped to mind. But I was Good Girl Thyme, extracurricular superstar and academic ace.

"Just to the Student Council," I responded politely with a smile. "And they are the *last* people in the school to do drugs."

Concerned Parent laughed. "Of course."

18

Party Like You're 49

Between the 101-proof breath and the
occasional bits of drool, some
interesting words come out.
              -from *Leaving Las Vegas*

Overheard in the hallway, Mrs. Anderson to Mr. Phillips:

"I hate this time of year. I'm on a total NyQuil/caffeine abuse cycle."

"NyQuil to get to sleep, coffee to wake you up?"

"Yeah. Thank God it comes in different flavors."

"Have you tried Lunestra? It's supposed to not give you a hangover the way cold medicines do. . . ."

I didn't see Lida again in a way that "we could talk, later" until that Saturday—the night of Their annual holiday party. It was pretty swank; although I had been dressed up and made to serve since I was four years old, these days they also hired a bartender, a waitron who came with the catered stuff, and some additional staff to help with the clean up. Still, there I was with my bow tie and silver tray of bruschetta topped with crème fraîche, hijiki, and caviar, smile plastered politely on. Maybe it was a little more Joker-ish than usual this year.

Coats were thrown on the bed in the spare room downstairs, along with all the purses. Well, all the large ones. All the small, incredibly expensive Judith Leibers or whatever were dangled from skinny, tanned, and feral wrists, as well as the occasional big-boned, matronly ones. Also in attendance were the usual diamond tennis bracelets and hideous large gold charmy things.

But back to the purses . . .

A. Assuming I was ever invited to any of the Big Parties this season, there was no way I could go without some sort of stash.

B. I still needed stuff to trade for Ritalin,

C. . . .

Aw, fuck it. There was no **C.** I would have done it anyway. As a little kid I used to go through the perfumed, woman-smelling coats, the heavy, expensive things in fur or leather, and the matching purses to see how they differed from Mommy's. Sometimes, if there was a new kind of gum or something, I would take one.

Come to think of it, there might have been a new reason.

D. Because I hated these people.

These were who I was supposed to be when I grew up. Sort of rich. Sort of married. Career oriented, or family oriented—no, wait: these days *both* oriented,

with a high passion for each. Good clothes. Big car.
Sufficient etiquette. Familiarity with the parts of a boat.
McMansion with four bedrooms. Crazed workout habits
to keep youthful body. Crazy BOTOX to keep youthful
face. Eventual divorce anyway. Spiritual reawakening.
Big, loose tenty clothes, trips to the Caribbean, a house
on the Vineyard.

Death. Eventually.

Overheard at the Gilcrest party:

"We'd be just as happy if he got into Dartmouth.
Karen's sister went there."

"Personally, I think" *insert name of aging Hollywood
starlet here* "has completely begun to lose it. Remember,
like, when Meg Ryan began to age?"

"Delts and quads on Thursdays, lats and triceps
Fridays . . ."

"Oh, you should totally go to my guy! He's the best—
here, let me write it down. Also very free with the prescription pad, if you know what I mean."

" . . . nothing up there, not really. Just fucking elk. Why
not drill?"

"Himalayan Terrier. Want to see a picture?"

It was a relief when Lida showed up with her parents.
I was given a break and we went up to my room and
flopped on my bed. We were so close during those silent,

parent-embarrassed moments that I almost considered inviting her into my purse-fishing operations.

But then no, she'd take a lot of shit herself.

Or would she?

It was hard to tell with the new, pseudo–Indian EuroLida. She still wore my earrings, but had traded her army bag for a gold hobo.

"I have to go soon," she announced, sitting up. "Reg is picking me up and we're going to the City—Bungalow 8. Wanna come?"

It was intriguing. I had never been, and this would be a nice, comfortable introduction to the party life I was meant to have. But there were all those purses downstairs to be mined, and who knows when we'd get back, or if my parents would even let me go, and those applications to finish. . . . Talk about dreams deferred.

"Nahh, thanks anyway." I said, really regretfully.

"Oh, everybody totally loves these, by the way," she said, fingering my earrings. "I've been telling everyone you made them. Majjy wants a pair. She might call you."

"Cool." It *was* cool. But I had to vent. And Lida, as stoner friend, would be as tight-lipped as they came. "You know my Altoids tin? The one with my stash?"

"Yeah . . . ?"

"Someone stole it. And handed it over to the fucking *police*."

"NO WAY." Lida's mouth dropped and her sleepy face

woke up with horror and admiration. I think I might have

actually impressed her.

"No wait, it gets better—the PTA meeting I was taking notes at? They brought it out, like exhibit A about what Kids in the Community Are Doing."

"Oh my God. They don't know it was yours, I take it?" she added, stopping her laughter mid-peal. "I mean, you're still here and all."

Quick deduction. Maybe it was her own experience with the culture of illegal substances. I nodded. She began laughing again.

"Ho-ly. That's all fucking ironical 'n' shit." But she did the Lida equivalent of biting her lip—a quick, snaky eyes jerking side-to-side, then looking down at the ground. Easy to miss if you didn't know her for fifteen years.

"You know something," I realized.

"It's what I wanted to talk to you about before," she muttered, scratching her head nervously like a monkey: a look at Real Lida, beneath the posing. "I, uh, I thought I saw Suze with it earlier this week. I thought maybe you were giving her some, you know, stuff, or decorated another tin for her or something. But she never said anything about it. I kinda figured maybe it wasn't all on the, uh, up-and-up."

I stared at her.

"Yeah, um, so there it is," she added lightly.

SUZE stole my stash? Suze-best-friend-of-*fifteen*-years Suze?

I didn't know where to begin with my anger. "What could have made her . . ."

"Maybe she was trying to abort, you know, it," Lida said, shrugging. "Take a lot of pills all at once or something."

I tried to make sense of what my friend had just said. "She didn't tell you . . . ?" I asked slowly. "She *got* her period. Like, a while ago."

"What." Lida widened her eyes and said it as a statement, loudly. I flinched, even though the soft tunes of Mannheim Steamroller Christmas and high-pitched laughter probably drowned it out. Then her face softened. "What if, I mean, it wasn't easy? Maybe she didn't 'just get her period.' Maybe it was a serious miscarriage, or she had an abortion and didn't tell us. What if she was in a lot of pain and was stupid?"

"She still could have *asked* me. She doesn't know anything about dosages, or—*anything.*" But I couldn't help feeling bad. The anger didn't go away; it was just mixed with sadness and frustration. "This is all pretty fucked up."

"Yeah. Totally."

There was something in the tone of her voice that raised my—uh, Spidey-sense, whatever.

Suze could have sneaked in and told my parents that she was leaving homework for me or something. Honestly, I couldn't be certain that it really was still in my bureau right before we left for Grandma's.

The night they were over, Lida had been going through my bureau when she found those earrings. Suze was nowhere near it.

And Lida was awful quick to defend Suze after ratting her out.

Something wasn't adding up. Especially with Lida's latest personality change.

The shit of it was, I would never really know. Unlike the mystery books I used to eat up as a kid, there would never be a clear solution to this whodunit. I would just have to be satisfied with the fact that I wasn't caught. And be way more careful in the future. And never trust my friends again.

"Well, gotta go, I'll drink a Mojito for you," Lida promised, leaping off the bed.

"Remember when we used to drink the rest of people's wine at this party, years ago?" I asked, suddenly angry and sad and nostalgic and frustrated and pissed. Once we scored a half a bottle. The three of us split it, giggling. I think we were twelve.

"Yeah. Nasty, huh?"

She left with a swish of silk and promises of fun elsewhere.

I stayed on my bed for a moment, staring at nothing, before heading downstairs to the purses.

19

'Tis the Season

You think people don't know you're a
drug dealer. Everyone knows, it's
no secret.

—from *Blow*

Any average conversation at Ashbury High, early December:

"Did you get in anywhere?"

"No, I'm doing regular admissions. You?"

"Same here. Wesleyan, Middlebury, and Connecticut College—as a backup."

"I just finished my applications. Columbia, Harvard, Yale, Stanford, and Fordham go out today."

"*Fordham?*"

"My uncle/cousin/grandfather/mom went there. What have you heard?"

"Genevieve got into Middlebury early. You?"

"Dorianne's going to NYU early. I didn't know people even bothered for schools like that."

Well, from what people were saying, the good news was
that Celexa seemed to be helping Dorianne get off her
ass and get her applications in. Even more reason not to
sell her uppers.

College fever was at such a level that someone with
a surprising amount of spare time on his or her hands
covered the hallways with posters of Kevin at thirteen
years old (in retarded sweater vest and bowtie), with the
encouraging words: "SEND THIS BOY TO STANFORD!"
on the bottom of each one. There was little need for jani-
torial services to intervene; everyone took a copy home.

Kevin thought it meant he was popular.

I no longer slept normally.

Was I an idiot for not applying early? No wait, switch
that around: Was I an idiot and *therefore* didn't apply
early? Was it a mistake not even bothering to try? What
if this was *the* mistake? The one I couldn't afford to make
that would ruin the rest of my life? Grandpa Gilcrest said
that people only had room for three serious mistakes in
their lives. What if this was one? I was already a third
through my allotment, and not even twenty yet.

Exactly three nights were spent tossing and turning
before I gave up and went to Ambien when I could get it,
everything else when I couldn't. "Everything else" gave
nasty hangovers, though, and required uppers just to get
me to school on time.

"Hey, you want to hang out tonight?" Will would ask, often by note.

"Can't, PTA meeting." "Can't, homework." "Can't, got to finish my applications." "Can't. Really want to, though."

"What about Friday night? You *can't* be doing anything Friday night."

"I'm hanging shit at the senior center to make it all festive and Christmassy."

Our trysts were short, usually confined to immediately before and after school, lunch, and the classes Will cut to see me.

My first real boyfriend, and I was a *shitty* girlfriend.

"Hey, have you seen your friend Lida lately?"

Dave sidled up to me in the hall like a cartoony con man. Cartoony except for his shifty eyes—there was something way too realistic about them. I was sick of hearing about Lida. She was suddenly everywhere, suddenly beautiful, and suddenly everyone wanted to know about her.

"No, why? Your latest batch of hydro come in?" I slammed my locker door, ready to move on.

"No, I have to, it's just, I have to talk to her."

His voice caught—there was something definitely wrong. And, come to think of it, they had been an almost-couple for a while, but I hadn't seen the two of them together since her whole Save Tibet Free the Dalai Lama Wear the Tunics and Harem Pants thing began. Dave was beginning to look like a casualty of Lida's latest growth spurt.

"You guys haven't been hanging much recently, huh," I said, almost sympathetically.

"No, it's like she—fuck, man." He kicked the ground, chilly in his T-shirt and leather jacket. The emergency exit across from us was propped open so kids and teachers could sneak out for a smoke. If he turned his head right, I could see a wisp of fog in his breath.

What was it with stoners and not layering, anyway? A sweater wouldn't have killed him.

"Something—I think something bad is about to go down." He looked left and right up the hallway. "Look, forget it. If you see her, please just tell her we have to talk."

"Sure." I actually felt bad. Weird, because at best Dave was amusing, and usually just sort of a necessary evil in high school. The Stoner/Dealer.

Friday night at the senior center I improved everyone's morale (well, okay, just us volunteers') by bringing some eggnog, which someone—Sonia, I think—spiked with a little of the Captain (Morgan). We all got the giggles and became a lot less lethally perfectionist on where the cedar swags should bow down and on which doorways to hang the faux mistletoe, which ones the lights. Genevieve surprised everyone by pulling out a couple of joints at the end and we all sat around and took a drag, admiring our youthful attempts at Christmasizing Shady Corner Comfort Center.

(Meera abstained, of course. Even though with her cast she had a definite medical excuse for inhaling.)

As soon as I got home, Mom materialized in the doorway, blocking my escape inside.

At first I was terrified at her knowing look—were my eyes red? Was I staggering? How did she know I was stoned ten ways to Sunday?

"Your boyfriend Will just got caught by the police," she said flatly, somehow making it way more dramatic.

Guilt. Fear. Guilt. Outrage. Guilt.

"What happened?" I demanded, forgetting to come in out of the cold. Mom just stood there in the door frame, looking superior.

"There was a . . . *snowball* fight. Apparently *things* got out of control. He seems to have been responsible for lobbing an ice ball at a Hummer, cracking its windshield."

I tried not to laugh. I really did.

I covered my mouth and coughed instead, pushing my way inside. "That's terrible," I murmured, trying to stifle a fit.

"It's not a joke, Thyme," Mom said, slamming the door behind me. How is it she could tell I thought it was hysterical, but not that I was high? Strange, this parental clairvoyance.

"Oh, come on," I said, wheezing, shedding my jacket. "I thought those things were supposed to be impregnable. A fucking *ice ball* smashed it? No wonder the soldiers in Iraq were so pissed about them."

"Watch your language, young lady," my dad said semi-intelligibly from the couch, where he was watching the news and having a light beer. "And they should never have used Hummers as antiassault vehicles of war. If Congress had voted enough money for Iraq, it never would have happened. Don't blame the car."

"Antiassault vehicles of war"? Apparently I wasn't the only Gilcrest stoned that evening. I raised my eyebrow to get a better look at Dad, who had obviously succumbed to a number of other things before settling on his tasteless beer.

"I'm not sure you should hang out with him anymore," Mom called as I went upstairs.

"Message received!" I yelled gamely back down, before closing my door and throwing myself into the chair in front of the computer.

I e-mailed him.

what the fuck?!

Okay, my cavalier attitude aside, the guilt really did win out. If we had gone on a proper date, or I had invited him to help, none of this would have happened.

Fuck. What the hell was wrong with my friends?

The phone rang almost immediately.

"He totally deserved it," Will began without preamble. "Besides just being dipshit enough to drive one of those gas guzzlers, he threw a bag of McDonald's crap out the window. Right onto the ground."

Okay, I could see being angry enough to respond to that. It's like a double fuck-you to the environment.

I took a deep breath. "What happened? Did the driver get out and run after you?"

"Oh, you didn't hear?" He sounded genuinely surprised. "He didn't have anything to do with it. I don't think he had any idea what happened—the glass didn't shatter, it just cracked like a spiderweb. He swore and almost went out of control, but kept driving. *Tildenhurst* saw it happen—I was waiting for the late bus when a bunch of us started the snowball fight. But she couldn't figure out who did it. Kevin cleared her up on that point."

No way. *No* one was that much of a bitch.

Right?

"You. Are. Kidding. Me."

"Absolutely not. If it weren't so obvious, I'd be over at his house beating the crap out of him right now. Guess I'll wait till summer. Since it wasn't technically on school property or involving anyone at school, they can't really suspend me. . . . More therapy, community service, a fine, maybe a public apology—that last bit I sure as shit am not going to do. I'm on probation now—if something else happens before I graduate, they're threatening to send me to a detention home or something."

"Jesus, Will. Don't fuck this up."

"I won't." There was a long pause, as if he was preparing to say something delicate. He was. "I would probably stop, uh, dealing to Kevin. He's a complete tattletale."

Huh, I wonder how he knew about Kevin and the Valium. Maybe he was paying better attention in class than he let on.

"I really don't think he wants his parents to know about his little habit," I said, completely unworried.

"You really have this all worked out, don't you," Will said softly.

"What's that supposed to mean?" I snapped.

"I mean that street dealers could take a lesson from you."

"What?" I felt an anger headache come on, for the first time at Will. "I'm going to take that from someone whose hobby is vandalism and the occasional fight?"

"It's different," he said with that cool-guy-listen-to-me-I'm-right enraging calm.

"No, it's not," I snapped. "It's just that for some reason it *sounds* cooler. 'I'm going to beat the crap out of that guy.' 'He totally deserved it.' It's macho bullshit. Why is breaking other people's things somehow better than selling drugs to them to help them study?"

"*I don't care about other people,*" Will exploded. "I don't want you to get caught two marking periods before you graduate."

I was quiet for a moment, silenced by the strength of his feeling. For me.

"Okay, point taken," I said quietly. "You have a problem with my prescription drug issue."

"Issues. Taking and dealing are two separate issues."

This is where, if it had been anyone else in the world, I would say: "I'm totally in control. I know what my dosing is. I'm not hurting myself."

Instead, I whispered, "Okay."

And continued: "As soon as this whole getting-into-college thing is over, I'm calling it quits."

"All right," he said, sighing with relief.

Let's see if he could avoid any more damage for a month too.

Breakthrough on the Harvard essay. Dreams aren't deferred. They don't just *get* deferred, either. *Someone* defers them. *You* defer them. You make a choice and put off something you dream of doing. "A dream deferred" is a copout, an escape from blame.

When I was growing up—I mean earlier, at the beginning of my growing up—we used to get to the city for at least one afternoon before Christmas.

These days, we went to the mall instead. Mom took me and Grandma; I took a couple of over-the-counter diet pills to stay awake and keep my interest up.

In my über-sorta-caffeinated state, the mall was *almost* as glittering as Fifth Avenue. The kids in line for Santa were actually pretty adorable, and even the elves with their rubbery prosthetic ears seemed to be trying extra hard.

"Three dollars for a cookie? That's robbery," Grandma muttered loudly, nibbling on a freshly baked chocolate chip. She chased it with a pretty impressive slug of black

coffee.

"You say that every year, Mom," Mom said, rolling her eyes. Like me. When I roll my eyes after something she says.

"It's true every year. Three dollars. *Robbery*."

We were like those Greek witches or whatever, the three generations: the girl, the mom, and the crone. For a moment it felt very real, like we were a power together, haunting the otherwise happy consumers, a bit of ancient doom plunked in among the plastic snow.

And then I suddenly wondered: Would I be at the grandma end someday?

Only if I was lucky.

Then we passed the art store, one of the few almost-shabby, rarely inhabited nooks in this otherwise upscale mall.

In the window, like the perfect pair of red shoes, was a sketching kit. A spiral-bound drawing pad fit inside a beautiful natural beige leather cover that had little slots filled with pencils, graphite, sharpeners, and those weird artist erasers that are the wrong color. I imagined Will's thumbs on the cover as he held it, stroking the buttersoft leather. The pencils in his hand.

Okay, is that weird?

"I gotta go in here," I told Mom, dashing in before she could reply. She followed, catching up to me as I was ready to pay. Damn it.

"Who do you know who likes to draw?" Mom asked, still pretending I wasn't dating the Boy Who Broke Cars. And Bikes.

And wouldn't it have been easier for everyone if she and Dad just said, "We don't want you dating him"? Then we could have a big screaming fight and I could rebel. So much neater than this endless round of raised eyebrows, snarky comments, and disapproving looks. Grandma was doing her best dotty grandma impersonation, looking wide-eyed at all of the different paints, pretending not to listen.

"Will," I said, gritting my teeth as the credit card went through.

"I'm not paying for that," Mom said.

"Fine," I said again, trying to smile.

Think: cloves! Think: Christmas Trees! Think: little rosy-faced kids getting candy canes! Think: bells! Think: motherfucking CHRISTMAS! Keep it there . . .

"Do you need money for something?" Grandma asked, suddenly paying attention.

"No, thank you," I said politely.

"She's paying for this out of her allowance," Mom explained further. So unnecessary.

I came out of the store, crappy plastic bag swinging like it was a BIG BROWN ONE from Bloomies. Grandma and Mom toddled along behind me, swept up inevitably in my current of good cheer, my Yuletide, *which would not be diminished.*

Having found my treasure, I had no problem doing whatever *they* wanted for the rest of the day, holding their bags when they tried other things on (why is it grandmothers always need bras, anyway? And why does it always take forever?). But I wasn't really inspired to shop for anyone else, anyway. There was a body jewelry and mehndi kit I thought would be nice for Lida, but felt no real compunction to purchase it.

And then I saw a strange sight: a bunch of little Twenty-ites over by the fountain, talking excitedly with Dorianne—who looked less than thrilled. Intrigued by the communication between two species that never naturally meet in the wild, I cautiously approached them. "Hey, what's going on?"

"Did you hear about what just happened to Dave?" GPA #7 demanded breathlessly.

Probably not "early acceptance to Harvard." I felt my stomach turn over in anticipation.

"He got *busted*," she finished, both excited *and* smug.

"You don't have to sound so thrilled about it," Dorianne muttered.

"What? With . . . ?" I made a motion with my hand, I'm not sure what, somewhere between holding a joint and shaking a bag.

The girl nodded vigorously. "Like ten ounces."

I turned to Dorianne, eyebrow raised.

"Four dimebags," she translated. "Enough . . . for them to identify him as a dealer."

Poor asshole. He got caught and I didn't. Not that I'm exactly a *dealer*. I never do it with *illegal* drugs and almost never for money. It's just for trade. Ironically, Dave got caught dealing the only illegal drug still more popular than the prescription drugs every kid wanted (from me). Maybe because he looked the part. Maybe because he wasn't quite as smart about it as me. Maybe because someone narced on him.

"Oh, *fuck*," I said sadly.

"Instant suspension," one of the other girls (GPA #5?) fairly crowed. "And there's no way anyone's going to accept him now." She meant college, of course.

"Shut *up*," Dorianne said heatedly. That was new. Maybe the antidepressants were letting her speak her mind more. Or she had a crush on him.

"Well, it's true."

"How *old* are you?" I suddenly demanded, breaking every unwritten social rule of The Twenty. "His life is over. Don't fucking *celebrate* it."

"He shouldn't have been dealing," the first Twenty-ite said, eyes hardening. "He was a *drug dealer*. That's what you get."

I know I wasn't imagining it when she said that last bit meaningfully, giving me that look.

"Let's go," she said to her co-Twenties, who followed her like the sidekicks in some awful teen movie. It was kind of amazing to watch.

"Unbe*liev*able," Dorianne said, echoing my thoughts.

I couldn't believe I ever wanted to be with them, and
just like them.

She shook her head. "Poor guy. He was the only one who came to all my shows, you know."

Ah. That was the connection.

"Let's not have a wake for him yet," I said gently. "Maybe he'll get out of it."

"Yeah," she said, rolling her eyes. "Sure."

I was quiet for most of the rest of the shopping expedition; when Mom asked what was wrong, I said I had a headache. Mostly it was uneventful. And then we came to this fancy European design store, kind of like IKEA but with just the accessories and all of them much, much cuter. On one of the walls hung a lockable medicine cabinet in the shape of a cross. In the background, Muzak played "What Child Is This."

I laughed and laughed and laughed—and then began to cry.

20

Junkie

Matt Hughes, star of the hockey team, approached me the first day Dave didn't show up for school.

"Hey. Genevieve says you have stuff—what about Vicodin or OxyContin or whatever?"

While he stood there, puck in hand, grinning broadly, I was the one who looked back and forth to see if anyone was listening. Crazy, because anyone walking by would have seen hunkalicious jock boy talking to a member of The Twenty. Nothing going on here. Move along.

"How much do you need?"

"It's how much we need."

"The whole team?" I asked, trying not to goggle.

"I've got this knee thing and Mark's got his ripped

ligament and there's a million other little injuries—nothing

serious. Just need to play through the pain, is all."

Remember, this isn't West Texas and we didn't have steroid problems. Yet. But even so, our football coach was famous for driving his car out into the field the night after they won a game and, without a word, taking a case of beer out of the trunk and leaving it for them. Equally silently he would then drive off.

"I'll see what I can do."

"Thanks, Thyme. Your team and school appreciate it."

"Go Tomcats," I said weakly, but Matt didn't laugh.

I couldn't take Ambien all the time—it smacked of something seventies-ish and while I couldn't remember any exact nightmares, I always woke up cold and sweating. Guilt over Will. Guilt over, okay, buying and selling and taking prescription drugs. Less "guilt" maybe than "fear of getting caught." Fear of college: not getting in/getting in. Fear of losing my friends. Fear of having lost them. Fear of never getting away from them. Guilt about these feelings. Was I allowed to be angry at Suze for keeping her miscarriage from me? She was probably going through things I couldn't even imagine. Was I allowed to be angry at the way Lida manages to slip out of old relationships, personas, and problems, clean and untouched? Even if I wasn't the one hurt by it?

By the psychological definition, I was already

addicted to Ritalin. With my dosage figured out and a steady supply, however, I was fine. I didn't want to add another addiction. I had to kick the Ambien.

Maybe it was time to do something about all this guilt. Well, some of it at least.

I e-mailed Will that night.

I want to see you.

You're the one with the crazy schedule.

Name a day. I'll blow it all off.

Tomorrow. After school. Before dinner.

Where?

The Lantern.

It's a date.

• • •

"Hey!"

Will was already at a cozy couch near the fire, no making the girl wait, no sirree. Underneath the occasional bouts of vandalism he was one classy dude.

He was dressed in textured, almost vintage clothes, a white collared shirt under a sweater with a thin scarf

that made him look poet/artist/academic/that dude from
La Bohème or *Moulin Rouge*, take your pick.

Yummy.

I was doing the fairy tale little girl thing again, the big mittens and hat and bright red coat, big, comfy Nordic boots with the yarny designs on them.

"Wow," I said, grinning. "It's like a real date."

"Almost exactly like one," he said with a smile, and moved his stuff out of the way so I could sit down next to him. He didn't stand up to take off my coat, thank God; that would have been dramatic to the point of embarrassment.

"Merry Christmas," he added.

"It's not Christmas yet," I started to say, but then I looked around. People at the Lantern didn't talk, they *murmured*, like everything was a romantic assignation. Maybe it was. The fire crackled and the air smelled of cinnamon and smoke. Outside, dark and canyoned clouds had gathered threateningly, promising *something* later on that night. Tiny fairy lights framed the view out the window, twinkling discretely among undecorated pine boughs and swags.

"No," I corrected myself. "This is the most Christmas I've felt in years."

He grinned. "That's what I mean."

A waitress came over, so well trained that she treated us seriously even though we were the youngest people in there by at least a decade. We got hot cider

with cinnamon sticks long enough to use as straws—
which I did, even though it kind of made ridiculous
slurping sounds.

"They're sending Dave to the same shrink I'm seeing," he said, getting the gossip over first.

"He's not going to have to go to juvie hall?"

"His parents are fighting it all the way. This is one step
toward that."

"I hope it works out. I hope he's okay."

"Me too, but it's going to be tough. The state of
Connecticut is sick of rich kids not going to juvie hall. Er,
according to what the shrink told my dad." He took a sip,
like a panelist at some sort of academic debate, not discussing his own awful possible future. "I don't disagree—
but it would be nice if they focused on the cokeheads
and rapists and shit first. Here," he said, changing the
subject, done. "I have something for you." He pulled out
two beautiful presents that I knew instinctively he had
wrapped himself. Artist's eye for detail and symmetry,
manly smudges on the tape.

"For me?" I said, delighted. Of course, they would
never compare with what I got *him*, but still, hey. Presents.

The first was a CD—not a mix, an actual bought,
in-the-wrapper from a group I had only sort of vaguely
heard of (as you might have guessed from the lack-of-
beading, other things like buying music and listening had
dropped to near zero this year). The Killers. As I turned it
over in my hands, Will coughed—almost nervously.

"They, uh, their main song's video is like a *Moulin Rouge* ripoff."

"How did you know that's my favorite movie?" I asked, stunned.

He shrugged uncomfortably. "I just—you know. I don't know. They're a little over the top. Kind of like Pulp. I thought maybe you'd like to give them a try. Open the other one."

Imagine a boyfriend—yes, boyfriend—who knew you so well that he picked out music you'd never heard but probably *would* love.

It took me a moment to figure out what the second prezzie was; at first glance a frosty plastic case with lollipop-pink handle. There were *things* rattling quietly inside its internal compartments. But it wasn't until I opened it up that I realized that my life had gotten so crazy that I didn't recognize beads in their natural habitat.

"Since you don't have time to do this stuff at home anymore, I thought you could maybe take something this small to meetings or in the car or whatever."

Wow. Just, like, two of the most thoughtful gifts ever. E-ver.

I felt my eyes tearing up.

"Aw, don't do that." Will looked down at the table with embarrassment and up through his eyelashes at me like a puppy dog. A really hot one you want to kiss (me, that is. *Me* want to kiss. Not you).

I took out his present, also handwrapped by the giver.

Much, much more shittily.

"All right!" he said, instead of "you didn't have to." Chanting as he opened it: "PSP Web upgrade kit, PSP Web upgrade kit." Then it was his turn to take a moment to figure out what it was. He opened the leather cover and ran a finger down each implement, naming it under his breath. "2B, EX, 4B, white charcoal, graphite . . . wow, Thyme." He bit his lip. "No one's ever given me anything like this before. I really need this stuff too."

"Merry Christmas!" I said again, brightly. "It's like 'The Gift of the Magi,' without all the sad shit."

And then he leaned over and kissed me.

Full on the lips. *Working* the lips.

Like, if I didn't know better, he'd been practicing on the side.

He finished by lightly dragging his mouth across my cheek, nuzzling it a little along the way.

Shivers.

And then he took my hand under the table and squeezed it.

I wish I could have ended the scene there, with a kiss. And presents. And the happy realization that I was going to have a boyfried on Valentine's Day for the first time ever.

Instead, the café door banged open and Suze came in like a blizzard's groupie, slamming the door and bringing in a gust of cold air. All eyes were on her. And then us, when she headed over to our table.

As a pair of teenagers Will and I were obviously just tolerated at the Lantern, provided we were quiet and paid and tipped enough. Now we were instantly lumped into the usually despised "loud and consorting" type of teenagers. Dead embarrassing.

"I need to talk to you," she whispered through gritted teeth, not even acknowledging Will. Her eyes were red and distracted.

Face burning, I got up and went with her outside, trying to draw prying eyes away from our table again, the conversational version of a wingman. It really was cold outside, and I shivered in my V-neck cashmere. Across the street her dad was waiting in his green Cabrio, a little smile for me.

"What," I demanded, assuming it must be something *really* important, otherwise she wouldn't have looked so hard to find me. I had no idea what it could be, but everything from *she was going away to have an abortion* (because she had been lying about the miscarriage) to *an apology to she and her dad were flying to Rio because they found her mom there*—anything.

Except for what she actually said.

"I totally need some OxyContin."

"What?" Like a sitcom, I smiled and waved at her dad. None of this was really happening.

"I need some. Quickly. Now." She hopped like she had to pee. "Before the pain comes back."

"*What* pain?" I demanded.

"The pain of having to fricking live like this," she said impatiently, throwing her hands in the air. Less dramatic than usual Suze. More cramped. Hurried.

About to come down in a spectacular fashion.

Some say it's worse than heroin withdrawal. I don't believe it, but that's what they say.

She didn't even pretend it was because of the miscarriage.

"I don't have any," was all I said. When emotions overwhelm, I can never think of the right thing to say. I always revert to honesty for lack of anything else.

"Yes, you do. I know you do, we saw . . . ," she protested instantly. Then stopped when she realized what she had just revealed.

That she had seen the contents of my Altoids tin. Before ditching it in the bathroom trash.

But who was "we"? Her and Lida?

My eyes narrowed.

"Look, I don't have any money now," she whispered. "But, uh, I can give you this ring, or this bracelet, or whatever." She opened her purse and thrust it at me; dark, sparkly, expensive things nestled in there. "You could take them apart, make jewelry out of them," she said halfheartedly, making up an excuse neither of us believed. "Come on, take it," she pushed.

I snapped back into reality, personality regrounding, finally understanding what I saw, all of it: the purse the girl the red eyes the *want*.

At what point had she become an addict? Why didn't she talk to me about it? What else had she been lying about? Was the pregnancy even real? Where was she getting all her pills? Besides my old stash, I mean. There wasn't enough there to start a habit, much less support one.

I could have been suspended, sent to juvie hall, refused admission to college if they found out who the Altoids tin belonged to. After she stole it and ditched it.

Anger overwhelmed me, then replaced itself with disgust.

"You don't have anything I want," I said, and went back into the café.

21

I Know What You're Getting for Christmas

For the plumber in his saggy pants,
    another clogged-up drain
For the millionaire in the mansion,
    more money and cocaine!
                            —Nerf Herder

You want to know about Christmas?

Why don't I just list off all the loot I got. I mean, that's how people remember certain Christmases, right? "Oh, that's the year I got my first bike." "That was the year all my parents got me was underwear. And socks." "I remember that time! I got a new computer." Or, you know, Familial Incidents—like the granny who drank too much and started cursing out the French, or the uncle hitting on your college roommate.

Let's not kid ourselves. I got good shit.

And there were no real family incidents. Grandpa and I argued about various issues over Christmas dinner (hint: He shouldn't be living in a blue state). My parents

went to a lot of parties, driving home when They really
should have called a cab. One night Suze's dad had to
stay over, too drunk to find his keys.

And then Christmas was over.

I'll bet you picture that time of the year in New England as quaint and beautiful, sunlight sparkling on ice and skaters, a light fluffy fall of snow when it's aesthetically important, church steeples and snowmen and caroling parties.

Let me disabuse you of this notion straightaway.

The end of December and January are gray, heavily overcast days that feel like the cold version of a pressure cooker: Sounds are dampened and the sun can disappear for weeks. Weather spokespeople say that January is the coldest month, with freezing nights and thermometers barely reaching twenty during the day, but February is *actually* worse, because by that point you're just sick of it and it *keeps going*.

Two weeks of Christmas Vacation are like longer versions of school days without the distraction of seeing your friends and *with* the bonus of seeing your parents more.

If you're lucky, you have a car and get away from it all.

December 26 I was on the computer all day, desultorily playing with my new toys and e-mailing Will. Outside, the sky was—yeah, overcast and close; if it was summer

it would have been 100 percent humidity with birds falling out of the sky; instead, the big, dirty clouds produced
nothing but threats. The light never changed from sunrise
to sunset, making the world weird, gray, and shadowless.

Watcha doing

Playing GTA—the new one.

What level are you on?

It's not like that. But I've been playing it for, like,
six hours.

Come over and play with me!

If I had a car we would have been long gone,
Honey Buns.

I IM'ed Lida and we talked about Suze—but
she never admitted anything about the Altoids tin.
Genevieve pinged me, asked me what I was doing for
New Year's.

Then I got an e-mail from one of the Mega Partyers,
forwarded, not directly addressing me or anyone
really on his list. Someone from Lewis Prep was having a New Year's party. And I was one of the beautiful
people, no matter how anonymously cc'ed. Invited.

But between now and then were five gray days and no car.

I took this time to visit Meera. She was still hobbling around, trying to remain cheerful during the days she should have been skiing. Her room didn't belong in the rest of her parents' house; Federalist style and antiques gave way to a surprising amount of computer equipment, terra-cotta pots of (medically useless) plants, shelves and shelves of science fiction paperbacks, and *Star Wars* posters.

After pleasantries and gossip, I mentioned the Oxy-Contin (and it wasn't for Suze, let me add here).

"You're going to sell it, aren't you," Meera said, sighing.

"I might know some people who want to . . . ease their pain a little."

"My parents took most of it when I told them I wasn't going to take them—they keep a crazy drug stash for their own use. Along with Cipro and iodine in case of anthrax or a nuclear strike," she added, rolling her eyes.

Huh. So that's where her crazy came from. "Can you get it for me? I'll pay you fifty bucks for the bottle."

"Thyme, you're going straight to hell," she said, shaking her head. "Or whatever. You're probably going to be reincarnated into, like, a vole or something."

"Sixty?"

"You're as bad as a Ferengi. Or, no wait, as a spice pusher in *Dune*."

"Seventy-five?"

Her eyes widened a little. "It's bad Karma."

"So buy a fucking whale with the money!" I snapped, exasperated. "Look, take the pills from your parents. You'll be saving them from themselves—if you want to talk about Karma. Then take my money and donate it to some rain forest or whatever. It's win-win-win for all of us. Me, my clients, your parents, the baby seals . . ."

Meera gave a low whistle. "You are one evil mother."

But she took the money.

You might think that Dave getting busted—and the ether suddenly going stone cold silent about him, like he had fallen off the planet—might have encouraged me to *not* go to what would probably be a notorious party with a purse full of pills. I even had enough Ritalin and shit to last me a while. So there was no real reason. It just . . . seemed expected. I mean, it's why he invited me, right?

Will was away with his family at an aunt's, carefully monitored on one of the drunkest, most troublemaking days of the year. "It's like an intervention. With board games and relatives I hate." On the thirty-first the mail brought a sketch of me from the notepad I'd given him, with stars and geometric figures and weird lights spinning off into space like I was watching a dance floor, delighted by what I saw there. Weird and cool and incredibly good. I put it in my mirror. Is that egomaniacal?

Me, a reflection of me, and a picture of me? It just seemed like a nice place to put it where I'd see it a lot.

Oh, and remember the party at Genevieve's?

Imagine . . . something much, mu-*huch* larger. Beautiful people. All kinds of people. And not just high school students. Some were in college (my cousin *Hauser* was there: cool/not cool). Serious pound-the-rafters dancing in one room. Serious smoking in another. High or stoned or drunk or otherwise mentally incapacitated kids cannonballing into the pool (sure, it was heated, but the air temperature was still below thirty, even with the patio warmers). A surprising number of bodies in the hot tub, at least some of whom were topless. And bottomless. And, yeah, actually pouring champagne into the water.

There was a DJ with his shit set up in the corner of the living room, surrounded by the music geeks nodding their heads and flipping through records. Yes, I said records. There were lights. There might have been a fog machine. The glasses were *glass*, and the drinks were weird, premixed shooters of incredibly expensive tequila and salt and lime, more than occasionally done off of someone else's body.

Bodies wore spangles, wore Armani, wore jeans and bikini tops, wore leather, wore feathers and diamonds, wore stilettos, wore Birkenstocks, wore bare feet.

I tried not to gape, but it was hard.

"*Thyme*. So glad you could make it!"

Coming to me out of the crowd, arms spread wide

was Lida, her transformation complete. Kohl and gold rimmed her eyes, a rhinestone bindi decorated her brow, a silk shawl graced her shoulders. A hundred gold bangles covered her arms, and she wore a long, flowing skirt the color of wet flowers. My earrings were gone, replaced by long ethnic chandeliers.

It was really only a matter of time.

And why the hell was *she* welcoming me to *this* party? I was the one invited, not her. How did she get on the list?

She air-kissed me on each cheek.

"Uh, Lida." It was hard to mutter; the music was too loud.

Her eyes were wide and glazed. Where she vacated her seat, a hookah bubbled, and I don't think it was with that foul-smelling apricot smoke we once tried at an Egyptian restaurant.

"I didn't know you knew our gracious host," she said, as excited as if somehow we had accidentally bumped into each other in a foreign country at some prince's house. Well, I mean sure, he was as rich as an old-fashioned prince, but still . . . we lived in the same *town*, for chrissakes.

"Have you seen Dave lately?" Again, it was hard to be dry and acerbic at the top of your lungs.

She rolled her eyes and adjusted her shawl.

"He said he needed to talk to you before all this went down—I think he knew something was going to happen."

Lida shrugged again. "You deal, you get caught. He

knew the risks."

"I thought you guys were *friends*." I couldn't help getting a little squeaky.

"He's old news. History. Come on, let me introduce
you to some *new* friends." She grabbed my hand
and led me to the crowd around the hookah. "This is
Anand, Daryl, Palmer, Majjy, Bradley, and *mein host*,
Michael. You know Tommy," she added, a little embarrassed.

Except for one or two girls, it was a pot-addled sau-
sage fest.

"Hey." They nodded at me, dark- and fair-haired
alike.

"*Thyme*," one blonde, I think it was Palmer, *kept* nodding and looked at me through wise, slitted eyes. "You're
the one who parties, aren't you?"

Anywhere else I would have laughed at the corny—
and dated—line. But surrounded by the smoke and the
drinks and the talk and uncomfortable with the crowd, I
shrugged as coolly as I could.

"Anything on you?"

I pulled out my new stash, a plain white plastic
squeezy box, Japanese design. Very futuristic. Nothing
like the former tin o' bling.

"Hey, you're the one who made Lida's earrings,
aren't you?" A girl with surprisingly clear eyes leaned
forward to look at my own earrings. Majjy, I think. I

found I suddenly wanted to talk to her more, devote my full attention to her, discuss beads and wire and jewelry and anything else but the pills in the tin. Everything else was menacing.

"Yeah, uh, yeah," I said.

"Wow, you are so talented. I'd *love* you to make me a pair."

This could have been a defining moment, you know? There I was with a choice, as simple as if God or one of Tildenhurst's authors had carefully defined it in neat writing on the wall, no subtlety or subtext: talk with the girl about beads or talk with the boy about drugs.

And maybe this really would be the only chance I got.

But I'd already *had* a bunch of chances, hadn't I? I didn't have to steal the first bottle from Will. I didn't have to bait Kevin. I didn't have to go back to Genevieve. I could have bowed out at Dave's bust, without losing face; no one would have begrudged me that.

This was only one in a long line of chances I'd had.

I was just using up my allotment. Quickly.

"Sure, I'd love to," I vamped, still holding out the box. "We should, uh . . ."

Palmer or Bradley or Assmunch took my pause, the advantage, and my stash. He tapped it so five or six pills landed neatly in his palm. Without a second thought he popped them into his mouth and chased them with a shot of something clear and tan.

"Holy shit," I said in shock. They all laughed. There was what, a Valium? A Xanax? Some OxyContin? A couple of Prozac? What the fuck was he *doing*?

". . . that was over fifty bucks' worth of pills, you idiot," I said, hiding my outrage in the transaction, or lack thereof. Greedy, but believable. Better than naive.

"I'm good for it," he said with a grin, taking out his wallet and peeling out—yes, a fifty. Then he took out two more. "And the rest, too, if you want."

"No wait, let me see what she's got," I think it was Anand, said. "Trade you for something."

"Got any blow?" another one asked, vaguely interested.

22

Richest Junkie
Still Alive

Supply and demand is the name of the game
—Machines of Loving Grace

The in-between days aside, January is a party month.
If you don't believe me, just look at my database. And I
was going to all the big ones now.

Will never came with me. I guess sort of like the same
way I never seemed to be around when he committed
his weird, random acts of vandalism or violence. He was
pretty good after the Hummer incident—although the
contents of Kevin's bag (including his laptop, and the
contents of his laptop) wound up spread all over Horse
Barn Hill, as flotsam and jetsam for sledders to avoid.

Besides our usual dates and hanging out, we even
went to a couple of basketball games together, just like
I promised Hal. It was kind of fun, especially with Will
explaining all the rules so I finally sort of gave a rat's ass

about what was going on instead of just cheering when everyone else did.

I wonder what would have happened if we were like those codependent couples and spent literally all our time together. Things might have turned out differently.

"Valentine's Day *blows*. It's a Hallmark Holiday invented to siphon more money from the masses and to make everyone who hasn't got someone feel miserable."

I bristled slightly despite the cold, hands tucked into my own pockets. Will was declaiming the obvious, kicking the snow as he went.

"I know, I just . . ." I couldn't think of what else to say. I guess I should have expected this, but was hoping he would somehow come through. Like the guy I saw at the Lantern.

I wasn't asking for a lot. It could be something ironic and funky; one of those little-kid Valentines that you pass out in class, or maybe a really stupid sappy card with something else drawn over it in thick Sharpie, or even an ASCII heart e-mail. With *Star Wars* figures. Heck, I would have settled for a single fricking heart-shaped message candy chosen specifically for its dumb but accurate sentiment.

I tried a different tact. "There's a party tonight."

Wrong!

Now Will bristled, and he was far better at it than I.

"Oh, that would be fun. Hanging out with a bunch

of your rich spoiled brat druggy friends, listening to bad music while people vomit at our feet. *Très* romantic."

"No," I snapped. "I meant if we're not doing anything tonight, I might as well go."

"Thyme, I don't do Valentine's Day," he said firmly, with just a hint of pleading: *Don't you understand? I thought that you were the one person who understood.*

"It's just retarded," he added, blowing it.

A certain card with da Vinci's hands outlined in beads and Swarovski crystals was going to stay hidden under my bed, robbed of its special day. Maybe for his birthday or something.

"We can do something tomorrow," he offered.

"Whatever," I said darkly, kicking some snow of my own.

I was brilliant that night.

After buying a small heart-shaped box of candies and eating them all myself, my crafty mind pondered lazily what to do with the now-empty box; it was such an appealing shape and there was something so nice and sturdy and reassuring about the cheap pasteboard.

I made a spectacular entrance at the party, holding the box high above my head. Then I presented it to the crowd: taking the lid off, revealing the "candy"—a party mix of all the pills I could get my hands on.

They cheered, they clapped, a couple of guys actually picked me up and carried me into the room like I was in a litter, adoring hands reaching for my sweets. Even

Lida laughed, thinking it was grand.

Of course, the shit had to hit the fan eventually.

A couple days later I was called into the counselor's office. I hadn't been there in years—just a couple of times as a freshman, crying, unable to deal with the bitches everyone had become, unable to deal with the pressure.

She made me wait outside her office.

For twenty minutes.

I began to get nervous. There was no one else in with her; all I could hear was papers being shuffled around, the occasional dull clink of a coffee mug being set down. A spiral of questions began in my head: Why was I here? Was I only nervous because I was afraid she knew I was a dealer, or would I have been nervous anyway, normally? Did she ever make me wait this long? I didn't think so. I couldn't remember.

When Ms. Bentley finally opened the door and let me in, the look she gave wasn't kind. At all.

"Do you know why you're here?" she asked unpleasantly after not asking me to sit down. It was weird being on the wrong end of her emotions; she was all motherly and comforting and psychological before.

I shrugged.

"Yesterday Stephen Riordan tested positive for drugs. He's been pulled from the hockey team."

My response was probably shit stupid, but as I said,

honesty under pressure is one of my biggest social problems.

"Our sports teams test for drugs?" I mean, it was kind of news to me.

"No, his *parents* tested him," she said sternly. Her hands had started out folded, but now one moved, almost casually, to a manila folder. It could have been my school records. It could have been his. It could have been her taxes. A prop, something else to make me sweat. "Some parents have begun doing this randomly as a result of what's been happening in other towns. They've taken him off of all extracurricular activities . . . along with other punishments."

Stephen Riordan . . . Come to think of it, I did vaguely remember his face among the grabbing hands. Shy, hesitant. Crap, it might have been his first time. Or was it the OxyContin that Matt was doling out to his teammates like a doctor?

I waited patiently. On a cop show, I would have said: "And *I'm* here because . . . ?" Smart-mouthed, guilty. Performing for the audience. In the real world, the less I said, the better.

"He was at a certain party on the fourteenth. So were you," she prompted.

"So were a lot of people," I said, giving in a little to the drama, a little to the truth.

She shifted in her seat. "You haven't been hanging around with the same friends you used to. I never see you and Lida and Susan together in the halls anymore."

Hah. Did you, Madame Counselor, know about

Susan's sleeping around, pregnancy, termination? Addiction? Lida's personality- and posse-swap? Just how good at reading teenagers were you, anyway?

"If you're going to get on my case about dating Will, like my parents . . . ," I began, hotter than I really felt, changing the subject with righteous indignation.

"I'm not talking just about Will," she said impatiently, cutting me off. "Although he *is* a strange choice for someone like you, with your crowd. I'm talking about other things, too. Too many people are starting habits at your age that are hard to change."

"Could you be a little more specific?" I suggested, thinking *lawyer*.

She fixed me with a steely gaze. "Please don't play dumb—there is a surprising drug problem here at Ashbury. You were at the PTA meeting, Thyme. Students don't take it seriously—like the sparkly Altoids tin. Like it's all a joke."

Huh, she noticed and remembered the tin. Did she notice and remember that I used to like to bead?

"You're beginning to hang with the wrong crowd, Thyme." She laced her fingers together to make one big fist, as if it would drive her point home. "I don't want one of our top students to be . . ."

"I'm not a top student," I mumbled without thinking, looking at the floor.

"What?" she said, surprised.

"Kevin. Genevieve. *Meera.* They're all top students. I'm. Not. Quite."

The counselor looked at me for a long moment. Before her mask of passionless social worker slipped back on, I saw a flash of something that looked uncomfortably close to realization/pity/sadness. If she made me cry, it was all over.

"Are we done here?" I asked, taking the offensive.

"Thyme, is there anything you want to talk about?"

"Sure," I said gamely. "How about how other high schools are getting rid of valedictorians because of the pressure on kids and the lawsuits from the parents?"

I'd read about it in the *New Yorker*, borrowed off Tildenhurst's desk. Who knew it had things in it besides inscrutable cartoons?

Ms. Bentley sighed, suddenly looking defeated. "Thyme, I'm keeping an eye on you. You only have a little more time before you go away from here forever. Don't screw it all up now."

This was a new development, one that I hadn't anticipated anywhere along my journey except at the very beginning, my first doses of Ritalin: adults not trusting me. *Suspecting* me. Losing the Altoids tin put me into abject fear and panic of the immediate consequences, not the eventual ones. The subtle ones.

I hadn't been caught doing anything, and yet had still somehow lost the trust of an Adult in Charge.

It was an . . . uncomfortable feeling. Thyme Gilcrest, star student, member of The Twenty, leader in many things extracurricular, being looked at through slitted eyes like a probable delinquent. Like, if she had *caught* me taking or dealing, then it would sort have been all justified. But without any proof I had still been moved from the category of praise/ignore to watch/suspect.

How did she know, anyway? *How* did she suspect?

Nervousness only lasts so long when you have a purse full of Xanax: It's an incredible relief knowing that any bad feeling you have will pass in twenty minutes. And yet I didn't take one. Partly because sometimes fear is good; it was teaching me to be careful.

But mostly I didn't do zanies because I wasn't one of Those People. The people I dealt the opiates and the downers to. I had my Ritalin; it was to study on; it had a purpose and a function and it was really ending as soon as I found out what college I got into.

I wasn't an addict.

And then Sonia Lansing committed suicide.

23

They caught it before we did, the news announced over the PA system. The principal's voice actually shook as she went off-script and gave a few details. *Well-liked senior and National Honor Society member . . . Passed away . . . found this morning . . .* A slip: *No one knows why . . .* She recovered herself: *The counselor's office would be open door all week, there would be an assembly, please, please, please come talk to them or your parents or one another at least.*

You might remember Sonia from my database, or a mention of her here and there. The barbecue host extraordinaire. Spiking the eggnog at the senior center. A bit part in the Life of Thyme. Someone I sold to occasionally, hung with rarely, and wasn't really chummy with.

I know what you're thinking, by the way.

And if this were a movie or show on Lifetime you'd be right: After overdosing on a pile of pills I had sold her (or having looked at what a horrible mess her life had become because of the drugs I had sold her), Sonia had become unspeakably depressed and killed herself.

Along with the corollary: I would come to the horrified conclusion that what I was doing was wrong and it destroyed people's lives, and I would stop doing it with a tearful admission and apology to everyone, and go to some state school to become a social worker, trying to fix the Many Wrongs I had perpetrated.

And although it was the beginning of the end of Thyme the Dealer, it didn't happen that way at all.

No, Sonia was just depressed. And killed herself. Just another teenage suicide you read about in the paper—or not. Quiet because it wasn't with an AK-47, taking out half the class with her. She had been depressed for a while, was even on Zoloft, but apparently no one knew the real extent of her mental state, not her friends (say it with me), not her parents, not her teachers, *not* the all-seeing all-knowing school counselor. "She was a quiet girl." "She seemed happy." "She loved taking care of her rabbits, Max and Ernst."

There *was* some question about the Zoloft, of course. It's famous for "giving kids suicidal thoughts."

But here's the real ironical part . . .

• • •

Overheard in the hallway, just hours after the announcement over the school PA:

"Did you hear about the empty bottle of Adderall they found in her room?"

"I didn't know she had ADD."

"She was taking, like, four times the dose you're supposed to."

"I heard they think she suddenly ran out—isn't withdrawal like that supposed to cause clinical depression? Maybe that's why she did it."

Yes, I sold to her.

Not all the time. But sometimes.

English class didn't let out early so much as just sort of dissolve.

"Were you guys friends at all?" Will asked, knowing it sounded dumb. There was a strange light in his eyes, as if he was about to cry. Wide, like he didn't know what to do with them.

"Not really. But I've known her forever—we were in Girl Scouts and ballet," I said, trying to recall every important image of her, every memory of interaction. "Our moms carpooled sometimes. She never smelled funny."

Will barked out a single harsh laugh.

"No, I mean, really," I said a little defensively. "You know how when you're a little kid and the worst thing you can say to someone is 'you stink'? And how other people's houses smell funny? She wasn't a close friend of mine or anything, and we had to share the backseat on hot, sweaty days in those ridiculous outfits. Spandex and scratchy acrylic stuff. I just remember noticing, Oh, she just sort of smells like a nice shampoo. That's kind of rare in little kids, you know?"

Will wiped his face; we both pretended it was from laughing too hard. "No, I know exactly what you mean."

"I shouldn't," I said as my own tears began. They popped full-formed over my eyes like contact lenses, and then melted, streaming down over my face. It was happening all over the school, but it was just happening to me. "I didn't know her, really. I don't have the right."

Will hugged me, right there, in the hall. I snorted my tears up through my nasal passages, much rougher than ground-up Ritalin.

The real sobbing didn't begin until I got home. I hunted through old closets and boxes until I found my sash, the one with the merit badges on it. She would never dig out her own sash again, in college for a sexy Halloween outfit, or to show her kids, or to share with a husband.

Adventure Sports. Folk Arts. Horse Rider. *Jeweler.* I held the rough cloth in my hands and began to weep.

I thought about that hour that I wanted to kill myself; *anything* to make the pain go away. I might have, too, if

I had been a different person. If I'd had a gun or a knife in my hand.

I wasn't. I didn't.

Sonia did.

"Is everything all right?" my mom called, knocking on the door tentatively with her knuckles in the way that I hate.

"Yeah," I managed to blurt out.

And that was enough. She was gone.

I wondered how long she was dead, lying in the bathtub with her wrists slit, before anyone noticed.

Everyone was invited to the funeral. Her bereaved parents wanted as many of her friends and acquaintances from school to be there as possible, dressed up and mourning, like a prom just for her. Oh, that's unfair. Most of us were there out of sadness and solidarity. A few—no naming names—overdid the dressing-for-a-funeral thing, long-sleeved little black dresses and hats and heels. I dressed like for church, but in more somber tones.

The cemetery seemed warmer than the rest of Ashbury.

Sonia's parents were open with their grief, unusual in our community. Her dad didn't try to manfully hold things back, her mom didn't delicately dab her cheeks with a tissue. Their faces were bloated and red, and one or the other would often turn away, weeping, falling into the arms of the nearest person. Sonia's best friend, Adrienne,

stood with them, her hand on the shoulder of the younger
brother who was shocked into silence.

He never took his eyes off the grave.

I could see into his head: willing the ground to open
up and his sister to come out again. It happens in horror
movies. It happens on TV shows like *Buffy the Vampire
Slayer*. Why can't it happen now? In real life? When the
person is a good person? When it matters?

Meera also never took her eyes off the grave. She
was there alone, and she stared. I don't think she blinked
the entire time, as if she was processing it in the computer circuits of her brain.

Suze and Lida came, instinctively hanging out
around me like nothing had ever happened between
us this year. Crying (dramatically), Suze put her arms
around me and squeezed. This wasn't really the reunion
I wanted or expected, but Will looked politely away and
I decided for the sake of the dead to let all things drop, at
least for now.

Rest now that we've all declared Peace.

For a moment the crowds changed and parted, relatives went to be with other relatives, and Adrienne was
by herself. Not even crying, exactly. She just shook her
head and looked at the coffin with disgust, like it wasn't
supposed to be there. I barely knew her, but she seemed
so forlorn and abandoned that I had to go to her.

"Hey," I said softly. "I am so sorry."

She blinked at me a few times, barely registering my presence. Then she completely surprised me. "Oh, thank God you're here, Thyme. I was looking for you." She grabbed my hand. The hope and enthusiasm that suddenly lit her eyes made me uneasy. "What do you have with you?"

The words she spoke meant nothing to me.

"What?" I said after a moment.

"What *stuff* do you have with you?" She widened her eyes meaningfully, pointing them at my little black purse.

"What are you talking about?" I said slowly, finally understanding what she meant. "You want pills? *Here?*"

"I'm . . . kind of having a hard time with this," she said, sucking back some tears and snot. "I feel like . . . the bottom dropped out. There's *nothing*. It's just . . . I can't deal with it. I need to dial down the pain."

A shiver went up and down my spine that wasn't like my usual rage—something far more spooky. I probably should have kept my mouth shut. Unfortunately for me, again with the honesty thing.

"Adrienne," I said slowly. "*Your best friend just died.* You're supposed to feel like shit."

"Not *this* bad," she said, eyes wide and looking lost. I wished I had something better to say.

"It's okay," I lied, squeezing her hand.

Nice moment, right? Like so many things in my life, it should have ended there.

Her voice turned hard, her eyes cold. "So you're saying you're not going to give me any."

"I don't think that would be a good idea," I said, trying
to sound adult.

"I can pay you later." Disgustedly, she pulled her
hand out of my own. Like I had somehow made the
whole thing tawdry. Cheap and gross.

"This isn't the answer," I said softly. "It won't fix anything. You're supposed to be sad. This will just . . . put it
off."

What I wanted to say was, *Hey jackass, your best
friend is dead probably because of pills. You really
want to follow in her footsteps?*

Or: *You think taking shit at her funeral is a good
memorial?*

But I'm a wimp.

It probably wouldn't have mattered anyway. She
turned from me angrily and stalked back to the crowd,
to the closest friendly face, shooting me a look that could
have taken out an army.

I rejoined my own friends, dazed and confused.
Maybe that's why I didn't notice Will's cold glance, or
Suze and Lida exchanging a meaningful nod.

The priest said some words, short and appropriate;
most of the talk was by friends and relatives. Adrienne
didn't make it very far into whatever she had prepared
before giving up.

I didn't pay attention.

I watched my colleagues: friends and not-quite-friends and acquaintances and strangers from Ashbury High, lined up in black, silent but not entirely pale (from annual snowboarding trips to Aspen or Jackson Hole). I looked into each of their faces, searching for telltale signs.

How many of them were stoned? Right then?

And I don't just mean on pot or booze. How many had rifled through their parents' medicine cabinets for Xanax or Valium that morning? Or OxyContin or codeine or Vicodin for something that wasn't quite a high, but at least wouldn't let them face this day normally? "Dial down the pain a little"? And how many were like me, jittery with Ritalin, still dosing themselves even though the hardest parts were over?

Scratch that.

How many were *exactly* like me, honestly believing that your brain and body could be enhanced, no downsides, with prescription drugs that no doctor ever prescribed for us? How many believed that prescription drugs were safer than Ecstasy, acid, and coke because they were FDA approved? How many were like Will, medicated but misunderstood? Were bored, not depressed? Were just following in their parents' footsteps, learning by example the habit of pill popping?

If you took a sample from the pooled blood of Ashbury High that day, how many of us would be left on the hockey team?

I did a mental calculation, working my way through the database in my head. At least a third of the senior class were included on it.

How many of us, starting now, would go through our lives carefully medicating our way out of feeling anything unpleasant? From funerals to Thanksgiving to dinner with not-quite friends to supper at home when you know there's going to be a fight with your S.O.—or even work the next day when you can't stand it anymore?

As I put my rose on the coffin, I thought about all the people I had gaily diagnosed and prescribed. Genevieve, who just needed to grow the fuck up a little. Dorianne, who should listen to better music and discipline herself more. All of the faux depressed and here was one we all missed.

Will didn't speak to me on the ride home, but I didn't notice.

He grunted sullenly when I asked if he would come in for a while. It was the first time I'd ever had him over. We were alone; my parents at work. I kicked my shoes off and sat on my bed, thinking about Adrienne, not Sonia.

"What the *fuck* was all that about?" Will suddenly demanded, yelling with the anger he usually reserved for mailboxes and assholes and bikes. Any other occasion, I might have shrunk back, terrified by the glowing coals of his eyes. But I was honestly confused.

"What are you talking about?"

"You fucking *dealt* to Sonia's best friend during her own funeral?"

"What? No. No, that's not what happened. She said she wanted some pills—"

"Yeah, which you just happened to bring to the occasion. To offer along with your condolences."

"Wait, no." I began to get angry. "I talked to her because she was all by herself and looked sad. She *asked* me for some shit. And I didn't give her any."

"Sure," he said, rolling his eyes. "Because that's just like you, Thyme. 'The epitome of warmth and human kindness.'"

"What the fuck is that supposed to mean?" I yelled, standing. "You don't believe me? *She* asked *me*."

"Oh, I do believe you. Just like when you said you were going to stop dealing as soon as your applications were in. You were going to stop doing Ritalin as soon as the second marking period was over, when it didn't matter anymore." He kept talking, but what I heard was *and remember how you "didn't really do pot"? And how you were never going to use downers to get to sleep? And how you were never going to try coke at a party?*

"*I didn't deal to her at her best friend's funeral!*" I shouted, trying to shut everyone up.

"Whatever." He crossed his arms and sat back, ass on my computer desk.

We were both silent for a moment, me working up the courage to tell him to get the fuck out of my room.

"That's what it looked like," he said quietly, looking at my desk, beginning to fiddle with things. *Like* an apology. You know, without actually being one.

"Whatever," I said dully, unbuttoning the top two buttons on my blouse so I could move my arms. Never in my life did I think I would be alone in my room with a hot boyfriend, undressing a little, without something like sex going on.

"Oh, Jesus *Christ*." He noticed the original bottle, brown-red, bedecked in beads. "Oh that's fucking great. A little shrine." He picked it up, eyes widening. "This was *my* prescription," he said, voice rising again. "You stole these pills from my room!"

"Yeah, maybe if you took them instead of throwing them away you wouldn't have been hauled into court again!" I spat, knowing full well I was in the wrong, and anyway, those were the wrong pills for him. If there even were any right ones.

He dropped the bottle on the ground. Just: dropped. Didn't throw, grind, or crush under his heel.

And then he walked out.

24

The End

I shouldn't have gone to school the next day. But I did.

You know those terrible days, when you walk into high school having committed some gross social mistake or thinking you have, alone, no boyfriend, no friends, no feeling of warmth or contact. Whether or not you really did anything.

In high school, hell is the not the absence of God, but communication.

Everything I thought at the funeral was magnified, through a weird fish-eyed lens that covered my head. Noise distortions howled in my ears. Everyone I knew and dealt to waved to me and I barely nodded. At least five were stoned already.

Well shit, they had been to a funeral yesterday, hadn't they?

I was misdiagnosed as having ADD for ten years. Turns out I was just lazy.

It's not funny. How do you go through adolescence with dulled sensibilities? What if your brain doesn't make those chemical changes they're supposed to? Like that movie we saw at Meera's house a long time ago, about a far future where everyone's drugged up. Totally unnecessary, right? We're doing it ourselves.

I thought about my journey from taker to dealer. Why *did* I keep doing it? It was fun being important and having something everyone wanted (and needed). Originally I sort of thought I was doing some good, dispensing my limited medical knowledge along with serotonin reuptake inhibitors and opiates to people who had problems.

I found myself missing math, veering left in the corridor when I should have gone right, heading toward the library. I read every pamphlet on the medical profession.

"Hey, Thyme."

I looked up—at some point I had not quite fallen asleep, head on the hard wooden table. Eyes open, staring at the inside of my elbow.

I blinked—the beautiful Genevieve was standing a little too close, dressed in shades of black.

"Uh, hi." I rubbed my palms into my forehead, trying to make myself human. I wished she wasn't there. "Can I *help* you?"

"I was just wondering if you had any stuff on you."

She smiled broadly, if a little nervously. No wonder. I wasn't responding like usual Thyme.

"So you can 'dial down the pain'?" I asked, just as dry and harsh as it sounds. "To help you deal with the *funeral*?"

"What? No. My supplies are just running low."

"I'm not dealing anymore," I said, stretching my arms out and yawning. I hadn't planned on those words, but as soon as they came out, I knew they were true.

"Oh." She looked confused for a moment. Then her eyes lit up with understanding. "Until this whole thing blows over, right? Because of her whole Ritalin thing?"

"It was Adderall," I corrected without thinking. "And no, Genevieve. I'm really done. Just done. Done diddly-done-done-*done*."

She was silent for a moment, pursing her lips. "You didn't make her kill herself," she said softly. I guess she was really trying to reach out, in her own weird way. Trying to make me feel better. You know, by suggesting that maybe I did. Make her kill herself.

"'We *all* made her kill herself,'" I pronounced facetiously. She didn't get it. "Never mind. Look, just forget it. It's over. Please go away."

"You can't do that," she said, biting her lip, finally getting just how serious I was. "What am I going to do?"

"Go see a real doctor," I suggested, putting my head back down onto the table. Closing my eyes this time.

• • •

"Hey, Thyme, I need to talk to you. . . ."

"Not now."

"Thyme—I'm looking to party tonight. I was wondering if you could hook me up."

"Can't right now. People breathing down my neck. You know what I mean."

"Uh, Thyme, you know our group presentations for English . . . ?"

"I don't have anything."

"Thyme, I need some stuff."

"Sorry. I'm out."

I spent a lot of the time hiding from people and reading books about careers in medicine. Notice I didn't say doctor. As I said from the beginning: I'm not that good at applying what little hard-won knowledge I have. The idea of organic chemistry frightens me; memorization and understanding are two completely separate things. And while the good news is that a lot of medical school *is* memorization—*oh, the thigh bone's connected to the knee bone*—the idea of putting it all together to diagnose an illness was a scary thought.

Also, I wasn't sure about the whole patient angle, and, more important, if this wasn't overreacting to a problem—going to med school just because I suddenly decided that my life as a dealer was making the people around me worse, not better.

I bit the bullet and made the decision to come into

contact with real live sick people. To test out my resolve. I went to the volunteer "fair," sad booths set up to entice kids who hadn't already figured out which after-school activities would propel them fastest to the best schools, do not pass go, do not collect $200.

"I'd like to sign up for a shift this summer," I announced politely to the underfrosh in charge of Candy Striping at Ashbury General.

Underfrosh cracked up, spitting a little between his braces.

I glared at him.

"Oh," he said quickly. "You're serious."

"Is there a problem?" I asked coldly.

"Come on, Thyme," the kid said, rolling his eyes. "You're a fucking *dealer*."

I went home and straight up to bed, lying on my back and staring at the ceiling until night.

Dad checked in on me when he came home. Unlike Mom, he opened the door without asking, stuck his head in. "Hey. Are you sick?"

"Not exactly."

Come on, ask me. If ever there was an ambivalent teen answer, that was it.

But he chose the wrong question.

"You need anything? NyQuil?"

"No thanks," I said, too tired to enjoy the irony.

But it got me thinking. Before I could even consider

treating sick people, I should start with a healthy *me*,
right? Physician heal thyself and all that? It would take a
while to ease off on the Ritalin without withdrawal, but I
could cut out the other uppers and downers right away.
Drink more water. Take the vitamins I always made fun
of. Something to boost my mental and physical state the
old-fashioned way.

After a while I came downstairs, got a bottle of water
out of the fridge and Dad's bottle of mega super bastard
vitamins out of the cabinet. I noticed as I tapped a couple
out that they didn't have the rotten tomato soup color so
many multiple vitamins did. They were a pretty pink with
little "20"s on them.

OxyContin.

That's what he had been popping for the last—oh,
who knows how long. Disguised as a healthy habit.

I slid down to the kitchen floor, laughing miserably.

My social circle dropped from one hundred to zero. Friday
and Saturday nights I stayed at home, alone. Lida was
busy with her new, glamorous life and I didn't bother calling Suze.

Genevieve tried to get in touch with me a few times,
pretending she liked me for me, but gave up as soon as
it was socially acceptable.

The spring months passed quietly. I kept to myself, her-
metic: When there were parties and school cut day and

graduation prep activities, I stayed at home or went to the hospital, where I helped people fill out forms and fluffed pillows and arranged flowers for the sick. My favorite part was when I'd get to read stories in the children's wing.

Harry Potter got me through March and April.

Mom and Dad only sort of noticed; maybe they were just happy I wasn't seeing Will anymore. I convinced them to limit my graduation party and dinner to family only.

They were only a little disappointed.

I got into Amherst, wait-listed a few other places. To my parents' disappointment and confusion, I took it.

I signed up for a few AP exams, not even sure if I was going to bother continuing French. It wasn't really necessary; Amherst has an open curriculum, and as much as I was planning anything these days, I planned at least on taking full advantage of that. At the exam for English, I was surprised to see—besides Genevieve, Kevin, and the rest of The Twenty—*David*, returned from the dead. He was standing by himself, holding a pen like it was a cigarette, tapping it occasionally, without thought.

"Oh my God, *Dave*," I went over to him. "What's going on? What are you doing here?"

"Hey, this poor cracker-ass convict's just trying to better himself." He slurred it in a surprisingly believable southern accent. "What?" he snapped, more Dave-like.

"Just because I didn't take AP English you don't think I can pass this shit?"

"Don't be a dick," I said, surprised at the words coming out of my mouth, the familiarity, the smile. "You know what I mean."

He immediately backed down, smiling a little himself. "I'm probably going to take a year off while things . . . uh . . . *settle down.*" He made air quotes. "But my parents thought it would be a good idea to get this shit over now, while it's all fresh in my head."

Kevin and the Twenty-ite he was currently dating, GPA #5, arm around her waist, had their heads close together, looking at Dave and me. Talking.

"What . . . uh . . . what's been the fallout?" I asked, trying to ignore them.

"A lot of community service. I wouldn't tell anyone else"—he leaned over close, looking both excited and embarrassed—"but it's cool as shit. We're working with these inner-city kids, taking them to farms and stuff, out in the country. . . . Dude, some of these kids have never seen a fucking vegetable garden. Can you believe it? And this one kid, he's never seen a tomato plant, right? But he makes coke into crack in his *bedroom.*" He shook his head, amazed.

I couldn't help smiling. It was a total cliché, but I knew that Dave was going to be all right. Not perfect, but all right.

Kevin and his little friend were rolling their eyes; I

saw the word "drugs" being mouthed. Yeah, it looked bad: The study drug girl leaping up to go over and talk with the pothead rather than her intellectual milieu.

A year ago I would have been with them, trying to fit in, probably making fun of Dave myself. It was hard to imagine. And here I was, 180 degrees and a thousand miles away, choosing to hang with the convicted dealer.

"Fuck," I said, shaking my head. I didn't fit in *anywhere* now. "I can't believe I used to be one of those douches."

"You were never one of those douches, Gilcrest," Dave said, surprising me. "You just took longer than everyone else to realize it."

"What, when I started dealing?" I asked dryly.

"It wasn't dealing drugs that made you cool, idiot," he said. Then he added, with a twinkle in his eye, "Though that was kind of hot."

In mid May, Will passed me a note.

I'm going to UMass. You?

I looked at him, confused at the sudden break of radio silence.

Amherst, I wrote back. Then: *We'll be neighbors.*

He sort of smiled.

• • •

The next week, he tried again:

Meera hasn't been in school for two days.

I had sort of noticed that too.

I called her parents' house, but she wasn't home sick. They thought she was at school.

He raised one of his fetching, beautifully thick eyebrows at me.

Then he leaned over: "Let's cut out of here and find her."

Old Thyme never cut class. Dealt drugs, yes. Cut class, no.

"It's a beautiful day out," he sort of whispered, ignoring Kevin, who was giving an oral report on Shakespeare's sonnets, in honor of spring (and yes, he was stoned on Valium). It *was* a beautiful day out, a blue somewhere between the sickly pale of humid summer and the scary dark of dry winter: soft, with soft sunlight, pollen in the air, apple blossoms decaying on the ground in drifts like old snow, tiny new leaves like the first time, in the Garden of Eden.

"Sure," I said. Seemed like a waste to be inside studying the Bard under fluorescent lights. In college, in the small classes Amherst promised, some grad student would probably take us outside on a day like this, not bothering to force subtext and symbolism out of brick walls.

As soon as English was over, we fell into step and left without speaking, exiting the famous smoker's unalarmed door. I paused and stretched in the warm air, feeling the sun on my face.

"Where should we start?" Will asked.

I thought about all the usual places people go when they cut: the mall. The City. The parking lot behind the train station to smoke and deal. The cafés on main. The record stores for the goths. The park.

Then my left-brain database zeroed in on the last time I really noticed Meera.

"The cemetery," I said softly. Somehow, I knew.

Will raised his eyebrow again, but didn't argue. We began walking.

When we talked, it was of this and that, nothing serious, who was going with whom to the graduation formal, were they really going to try a lock-in for the after-party like they threatened, how much shit we planned on taking to college with us, what kind of computer, how many thank-you cards we had to write for presents we didn't want.

"I sort of abandoned you at the worst possible time, didn't I?" he finally said, out of nowhere, the way a guy sometimes will. If the guy is Will.

"Uh." I pretended to think about it. "Yeah."

He snatched at a twig, broke it off, threw it. "I'm really sorry."

He meant it, which I guess is all that counted. Though a little late.

When we got to the cemetery, Will let me lead, not having made the connection yet. It took me a few minutes to remember where it was: on the top of the hill, with a nice view now that it was spring. And there she was, sitting at Sonia's grave, notebook and bag spread around

her, eating a sandwich.

"Uh, hi," Meera said, so used to being considered strange that she didn't even bother to be embarrassed or surprised at our arrival. "I was just catching her up on the homework for basic chem. I had to get it from Dorianne." She had to get it from Dorianne because *she* was in AP Bio, almost four full grades above basic chem.

Will was the only one really unsettled by it all.

"You two were, uh, friends?" he said, trying to sound cool, swallowing hard.

Meera shook her head. "No, not since kindergarten. But I figured no one else was going to."

I sat down next to her. Will followed suit.

"You *know* this is kind of fucked up, right?" I asked gently.

"Oh yeah," she said, shrugging. "But I figured since we'd probably never speak again after high school anyway, I could sort of let it drop naturally after graduation."

The three of us sat quietly for a few moments, enjoying the sun and the view. Meera offered us her Fritos and we accepted. She was going to Williams, having turned down a few Big Ivy Leagues for the "cool" monastic and gloomy atmosphere the mountains afforded.

She was delighted to hear we were less than an hour away; we could carpool.

• • •

So I ended my senior year at a much smaller graduation party than I'd imagined. While a blow-out to be remembered for all time was going down with the boys from Lewis Prep, I was at Meera's with Will and a few others from the science fiction club, stuffing ourselves with deviled eggs and chocolate mousse at a midnight picnic on her lawn. Mr. and Mrs. Meera poured very carefully allotted Dixie cups of champagne. We picked strawberries from the garden and dropped them in, sipping delicately at the resulting pink fizz.

At one a.m. they finally started the movie: *Star Wars*, projected on the side of the house with some equipment an A/V geek "borrowed" from school. Will and I lay on a blanket, watching it, and the stars, and the fireflies, holding hands.

Epilogue

Unpacking my stuff into their new places in the dorm room:

A few knickknacks on the desk. Toiletries into the basket for taking to and from the bathroom. Flip-flops at the base of the bed.

My roommate is (so far) not that cool and way too enthusiastic, but *very nice*. From Arizona with a *very nice* mom, a box of chocolate-jalapeño brownies, and an incipient eating disorder. Her accent is soft and long and she terrifies easily. We're going to a late dinner at the cafeteria and I'm going to try not to react when she grabs my arm while making a point. Which she does. All. The. Time.

In my old travel toiletries pack, something rattles in the base of my brush. I pop off the handle and sigh: two Ritalin. Just In Case.

I take it and everything else into the bathroom, planning to brush my teeth and drop the pills into the john. My hand is over the swirling, turbid waters, in fact, when two loud voices burst into the coed bathroom.

"I am *completely fucked*. I was so stupid for signing up for accelerated French. Are you sure you don't have *anything?*"

"Fuck no," the other voice said. "I'm cleaned out."

"Shit." Then, louder, to the bathroom at large: "Does anyone have any Adderall? Ritalin? Stratera? I'll pay . . . fuck it, I'll pay fifty bucks a pill."

I react without thinking, my hand closing, stopping the pills from their downward roll into the water.

Afterword

Fans of *Snow* and the Nine Lives of Chloe King series might be a little surprised that I chose to write a book like this. My reasons were purely personal: I know at least two people whose lives were ruined—and are being ruined—by their addiction to illegally obtained prescription drugs.

I wish I could tell you that it gets easier when you're older, that the worst years of "just say no" are when you're a teen or in college. Unfortunately, that's just not the case. Day traders buy their Ritalin on the street, and ads on TV sell us pills that, as Thyme would say, will cure your every fricking problem; adults are also constantly tempted by the quick fixes that drugs promise.

It may sound clichéd, but it's true: Learning to say no now makes it easier later.

I know how hard it can be. Believe me when I say more power to you.

If you know someone who is losing the battle against an addiction, please first try to talk with a trusted adult: favorite teacher, school counselor, parent, etc. For more information, check out www.freevibe.com.

To locate a treatment facility in your area, contact the National Drug and Alcohol Treatment Routing Service at http://www.health.org/referrals/ or 1-800-729-6686.

The one thing worse than having a friend who hates you is a friend who is dead.

Trust me on this one.

—Tracy Lynn

Acknowledgments

Thank you to everyone who was willing to talk to me professionally about prescription drug addiction, and who vetted the manuscript to make sure it was all correct. Any inaccuracies are of course my own. Tom Kovar, Dave Stern (for introducing me to Tom), and Dr. Richard Malen.

More thanks to everyone on LiveJournal who helped me with the songs for chapter titles: Darcy, Cecil, Mara, Holly, Jennifer, Monique, and, of course, Barry.

(Double espresso thanks to Barry. You really are the bestest agent ever.)

Thank you also to Scott for reading every draft, supporting me through every hard bit, and making all those cups of tea.

FINALLY, thank you Cheng-Jih Chen for administering my server, updating my blog software, blocking my spammers, and making my e-mail happen. For free.

About the Author

Tracy Lynn is a pseudonym. Liz Braswell is a real person. After the sort of introverted childhood you would expect from a writer, Liz earned a degree in Egyptology at Brown University and then promptly spent the next ten years producing videogames. Finally she caved in to fate and wrote Snow, her first novel, followed by The Nine Lives of Chloe King series under her real name, because by then the assassins hunting her were all dead.

Liz lives in Brooklyn with her husband, two children, and the occasional luna moth.